Faeries and the Natural World

JOHN KRUSE

GREEN MAGIC

Green Magic
Seed Factory
Aller
Langport
Somerset
TA10 0QN
England

www.greenmagicpublishing.com

Designed & typeset by Carrigboy, Wells, UK
www.carrigboy.co.uk

ISBN 9781838418588

GREEN MAGIC

Contents

Introduction

It is an article of faith central to fairy belief today that they are beings intimately connected with nature – they are the elemental spirits, even, of water, air and vegetation. In one form or another, this view has long existed.

Examining the development of faery belief in 1946, Lewis Spence wrote that "All nature spirits are not the same as fairies, nor are all fairies nature spirits. The same applies to the relationship of nature spirits and the dead. But we may safely say that a large proportion of nature spirits became fairies, while quite a number of the dead in some areas seem to take on the character of nature spirits." That said, he then went on to admit that only vestigial remains of true nature spirits can be found in the British Isles and that there are no 'genuine' tree or water spirits akin to the Greek dryads and naiads.[1]

In the decades before Spence wrote, the idea of faeries as elementals had gained considerable currency. This was the result of a conjunction between a variety of philosophical and religious influences. By way of Theosophy, there were substantial importations of concepts and terms from Eastern philosophies and religions into the traditional fairy faith. Additionally, fairies were accommodated within a hierarchy of supernatural beings that was borrowed directly from Neo-Platonism via Swedenborg and others. Theosophist and writer, Edward Gardner, typified this syncretic approach when he wrote in his Introduction

---

1   Spence, L. *British Fairy Origins.* (1946) pp110 & 113.

to Geoffrey Hodson's *Fairies at Work and Play* that "Folk tradition believes in fairies. The mystery tradition speaks of devas, nature spirits and elementals. There is *no* dead matter to the occultist."[2]

Synthesising these many diverse concepts together, Hodson, amongst others, identified a range of spiritual beings on an evolutionary ladder. The list of types in the hierarchy was not absolutely fixed, and there could be evolution from one category to another, but Hodson recognised a spectrum of types, which included *devas* – shining angels who act as the guardians of nature and help to develop the vegetable kingdom; *sylphs* – nature spirits of wind and blossom; *brownies* – beings associated with the soil and trees; *wood elves* – living underground around tree roots; *gnomes* – beings of an earthly character who inhabit gardens and similar green places and who may, under the influence of devas, evolve into fairies and take an interest in plants and flowers; these *fairies* are small, bird-like nature spirits who are found in fields and gardens supervising the building and opening of flowers. Lastly, Hodson identified a number of other, lesser nature spirits including *tree men, grass spirits* and *elementals*, which are temporary living creatures active in the vegetable kingdom. This list is an undiscriminating combination of traditional British faery beings along with entities derived from Indian mythology and the theories of Paracelsus. Nevertheless, it has proved remarkably influential in modern thought – for instance, in the view of the natural world enunciated at the Findhorn community.[3]

---

2 Hodson, G. *Fairies at Work and Play*. London (1930).
3 Pike. *Faery Tale*. p279.

Spence was writing a study of British fairy origins, and his consideration of faery-beings as 'elementary spirits' was predicated upon and shaped by his overall plan. Hodson and Gardner wrote within a particular intellectual and spiritual environment. Here, I'm not interested in trying to develop a folklore theory evolution and descent in human beliefs. Rather, I seek to locate fairykind within the world they inhabit and explain their functions and interactions within those environments. The faes are, unquestionably, part of nature and an active element within it. Their role within that complex web is my focus in this discussion.

CHAPTER ONE

Naturist Fairies

There is a very widespread and longstanding convention to portray fairies as naked (and, for that matter, as young and as female). If we accept the idea that they are wild beings living a natural existence in the countryside, their want of clothes need not surprise us particularly. The faeries are as naked as they were born and, in that respect, are no different from any of the other creatures with which they coexist.

However, the faeries' 'natural' state in artworks produced over the last two centuries – imagery which has proved extraordinarily influential upon our perceptions of the 'typical' faery being – is a product of social and aesthetic forces and is not necessarily reflective of British faery belief. In a study published in 2017, American art historian Susan Casteras contributed a chapter on Victorian fairy painting. In this, she perceptively remarked how nudity, which is very far from being an inherent element in folklore, became something that the Victorians chose to exaggerate in their visions of fairyland. Many paintings of the period, she rightly observed, were all about "flaunting nudity for its own sake rather than as a supposedly accurate transcription of faery lore."[1]

---

1 Casteras, S. 'Winged Fantasies: Constructions of Childhood, Adolescence and Sexuality in Victorian Fairy Painting' in Marilyn Brown. *Picturing Children* (2017). c.8, pp127–8.

Looking at the work of Victorian artists like John Simmons, you cannot help but agree with the second part of Casteras' comment. Admittedly, Simmons was a particularly egregious offender, producing a number of 'pin-up' canvases, but his work typifies a view of Faery that prevailed in the mid- to late-nineteenth century period and which is still highly influential today, as we may witness in the works of modern painters and illustrators such as Alan Lee, Brian Froud and Peter Blake. We have become habituated to the idea of a Faery full of frolicking nudes, but how traditional is this? What exactly is the British folklore evidence?[2]

The honest answer is that there's very little sign of nudity in the older accounts of Faery. Nakedness is fairyland is very rare indeed. One of the few stories in which it features, obliquely, concerns a little girl who temporarily went missing in Devon. A gamekeeper and his wife living at Chudleigh, on Dartmoor, had two children, and one morning the eldest girl went out to play while her mother dressed her baby sister. In due course, the parents realised that the older child had disappeared and several days of frantic and fruitless searching followed. Eventually, after hope had nearly been lost, the girl was found quite near to her home, completely undressed and without her clothes, but well and happy, not at all starved, and playing contentedly. The pixies were supposed to have stolen the child, but to have cared for her and returned her.[3]

Now, this girl was a human infant and there may have been several reasons why the pixies might have taken off all her clothes. They may have objected to human things;

---

2 See my *Twentieth Century Faery Art* (2020).
3 Northcote. 'Devonshire Folklore,' *Folklore*. Vol.11. (1900) p213.

they may have thought that a 'natural' unclothed state was healthier and preferable. Whatever the exact explanation, it's one of the few instances where there's a suggestion that nudity might be the normal condition in Faery. Another example concerns an adult. A woman in Argyllshire went missing for two months and, despite searches, her husband was unable to find any trace of her at all. One day, he was walking in a wood near their home when he heard her voice calling to him from a hazel bush. She was concealed there and told him that she had been in Faery but was now tired and wanted to come home. However, the fairies had taken all her clothes, so he had to return every day with an item for her until she had a full outfit again and was able to escape the fairy thrall and get back to him and their children. From this account, it seems that stripping the abductee was part of the process of securing her in Faery and that recovering her human garments somehow facilitated her liberation. Lastly, as we shall read much later in the book, a group of people in Wales in 1760 saw some flying faery beings, who – to some of the witnesses – looked like naked babies.[4]

The rest of the available evidence is all qualified in one way or another. Mermaids don't have clothes, but that's for very obvious reasons. Men are forever falling in love at first sight with these creatures, but you may well suspect that coming across an uninhibited and naked female is a pretty strong draw in any case. The same may be said of several of the faery maidens encountered in medieval romance. These females set out to entrap human males and they do so by allowing themselves to be found bathing

4   Cartwright, M. 'Collectanea: Argyllshire,' *Folklore*. Vol.21. p90.

in woodland fountains or relaxing in a state of undress on a hot summer's day.[5]

Some fairies don't 'need' clothes at all because they're naturally very hairy: the brownies, hobgoblins and the Manx fynoderee are all examples of these. Their shaggy pelts are covering enough. It's almost always this kind of faery that is the subject of a story in which a reward of clothes for services rendered alienates the helpful being. Typically, a brownie or boggart will work faithfully on a farm, threshing grain, carrying hay and tending the livestock, all for very little reward except some bread and milk left out at night. After a while, the curiosity of the farmer overcomes good sense and the creature's labours are spied upon. It's seen to be (at the very best) dressed in tattered rags or (at the worst) completely naked. Pity is taken and new clothes are made in recognition of its hard work, but all that's achieved is to offend the fae, who recites a short verse – and leaves forever. As may be the case in respect of the Chudleigh girl, human clothing could be inherently objectionable to fairykind, which is why brownies take such umbrage at the well-meaning gifts.

Although not entirely their invention, nude fairies seem to have been very much largely a Victorian obsession; they are the soft porn of their day. It was acceptable to display bare breasts in art, but only so long as it was justifiable and/or distant from the present day. Painting academic studies of classical nymphs, or depicting exotic oriental harems and fairyland let artists get away with it. They seized the opportunity – regardless of the fact that the folklore provided almost no basis for this.

5 See my *Beyond Faery* (2020), chapter 1; and *Love & Sex in Faeryland* (2021).

It is very likely that these images informed later imaginings of faery – just as they in their turn seem to owe a considerable debt to the medieval concept of the available and alluring fae maid. It's notable how in the 1920s Geoffrey Hodson waxed lyrical about the young girlish figures of the devas, fairies and tree spirits he encountered. Undines and sea fairies, for example, are reported to be "always nude ... [their forms] always entrancingly beautiful." More often, their fresh, slender, schoolgirl bodies could be glimpsed through the thin white drapery they wore. Even so, most of Hodson's brownies and gnomes were clothed. The main exception to this was the wood elves who, as Hodson states, "Differ from other nature spirits chiefly in that they do not appear to be clothed in any reproduction of human attire, and that their bodily constitution appears to consist of one solid mass of gelatinous substance, entirely without interior organisation." He saw two of these jelly-like figures in a wood near Cottingley in August, 1921. These creatures might be regarded as 'nude', but their form is so different to ours that it is not really an apt term.[6]

Aside then from these strange reports and the fantasies of painters, British faery beings are almost uniformly clothed. The cases where they are discovered nude seem always to be explicable by some untoward event. In this respect, therefore, they are not part and parcel of nature, like the insects and birds, but are set apart by their civilisation – just as human beings are. They may live in natural surroundings, but they are not naturists.

---

6 Hodson, G. *Fairies at Work & Play.* cc.1, 2, 4 & 7; *Kingdom of Faerie.* (1927). c.4 & 6.

CHAPTER TWO

Faeries and the Land

Lewis Spence in his landmark book, *British Fairy Origins,* stated that "The association of fairies with agriculture is important. That they retained the ownership of all waste land until it was cleft by the spade is generally accepted as genuine folk belief." Elsewhere, he identified an even deeper and perhaps more ancient connection, saying that the *sith* folk of the Scottish Highlands were "a mixture of tumulus dweller and wood nymph." They represent the spirits of the ancient dwellers upon the land, as well as embodying the natural life of that country.[1]

The faeries' inhabitation of – even identification with – the landscape of Britain dates back many centuries. Several Anglo-Saxon glossaries contain lists of terms that describe the various types of elves that will be found in the country, classified by where they dwell. Whilst it is true that a few of these terms may be translations from Greek words such as oread and naiad, several others are wholly English expressions and indicate the wide range of environments within which the Saxons expected to encounter elves. The manuscripts list *dun-ælfen, munt-ælfen* and *berg-ælfen* (hill and mountain elves), *feld-ælfen* and *land-ælfen* (field elves), *wæter-* and *sæ-ælfen* (water and sea elves) and, lastly, *wudu-ælfen* (wood elves). Essentially, every possible habitat was invested with supernatural life.

---

1 Spence, L. *British Fairy Origin.* (1946) pp30 & 7.

Another indication of how closely faes and the land may be linked – and how very old that association may be – comes from the north of Scotland. Renowned folklorist, John Gregorson Campbell, recorded that the faery diet, over and above the meat and dairy products that they stole from humans, consisted of a range of wild products. Before there was agriculture, they subsisted upon "food peculiar to themselves and not acquired from men, [such as] the root of silverweed (*brisgein*), the stalks of heather (*cuiseagan an fhraoich*), the milk of the red deer hinds and of [wild] goats, weeds gathered in the fields, and barleymeal." Campbell explains that *brisgein* is "a root plentifully turned up by the plough in spring [which] ranked in olden times as the 'seventh bread'. Its inferior quality and its being found underground are probably the cause of its being assigned to the fairies. It is a question whether the stalks of heather are the tops or the stems of the plant. Neither contain much sap or nourishment." This may sound like quite poor food, but it implies nonetheless that the faeries have been dwelling on the land for millennia and had become familiar with its resources long before human farmers ever appeared. In addition, the Scottish pixies known as the *pechs* are celebrated for the heather ale they used to brew. Yet another indication of the intimate reliance of the faes upon the land, or the integration of the culture to its natural resources, is the practice of the *sith* folk of the northern Hebrides to dye their clothing with a locally available lichen, called *crotal* in Scottish Gaelic. Because of this, the *sith* are usually referred to in this area as 'little red men,' (*daoine beaga ruadh*) reflecting the colour produced by the plant.[2]

2 Campbell, J.G. *Superstitions*. p14.

The Welsh *tylwyth teg,* meanwhile, demonstrate an identical closeness to the land. They are reported to live on fruit, flowers, nuts, honey (and cream, which can be left for them in their rings). They reportedly dye their clothes with whinberries.[3]

SPIRITS OF THE LAND

In his introduction to the 1974 reprint of Alfred Watkins' ley line classic, *The Old Straight Track,* John Michell noted how both Watkins and the Reverend Francis Kilvert invoked the "same *genius terrae britannicae*" of the red Herefordshire earth. This *genius,* the 'spirit of the British land,' is very much what we are describing when we discuss British fairies.

During the 1920s and '30s, the painter Paul Nash sought in his work to discover and free this imprisoned spirit, the motive power that animated the British landscape. He deeply felt that a spirit of place, a *genius loci,* inhabited the soil and scenery and that certain poets in particular sensed it. William Blake, he felt, "perceived among many things the hidden significance of the land he always called Albion."[4]

Elsewhere, Nash wrote that "The idea of giving life to inanimate objects is as old as almost any record or fable. It has varied in its conception throughout very different histories," which unquestionably include fairy lore and mythology. This "endowment of natural objects, organic but not human, with active powers or personal influences"

3 *Welsh Outlook.* Vol.14, No.10 (October 1st 1927); Vol.16, No.10 (October 1st 1929). p297
4 Personal Statement. *Unit One.* (1934).

lies at the core of faery belief, I also believe.[5] When Nash wrote the lines just cited, the artist had recently visited the Avebury stone circle for the first time and it had evidently impressed him deeply. He continued that "it is not a question of a particular stone being the house of the spirit – the stone itself has its spirit; it is alive." This idea of animating inanimate objects was very old indeed, "a commonplace in fairy tales and which occurs quite naturally also in most mythologies." Sketching at Silbury Hill near Avebury, Nash recalled that:

> "I felt that I had divined the secret of that paradoxical pyramid. Such things do happen in England, quite naturally, but they are not recognised for what they are – the true yield of the land, indeed, but also works of art; identical with the intimate spirit inhabiting these gentle fields, yet not the work of chance or the elements, but directed by an intelligent purpose ruled by an authentic vision."

Earlier writer, Maurice Hewlett, had had the same perception as Nash. In his 1913 novella, *The Lore of Proserpine,* he recorded how "I have seen spirits, beings… and have observed them as part of the landscape, no more extraordinary than grazing cattle or wheeling plover." A little later, he added that he regarded them as a "natural fact … a part of the landscape."[6]

As just seen, Nash discussed the 'yield' of the land. This term suggests that, almost like crops or the native fauna and flora, the faery folk are a product, a natural outgrowth of the soil. In addition, I think we can usefully borrow a

---

5 Nash, P. 'The Life of the Inanimate Object,' *Country Life* (May 1st 1937).
6 Hewlett, M. 'The Soul at the Window,' *The Lore of Proserpine* (1913).

further term from English land law and talk about the 'burden' of the land: this is a term denoting certain costs or obligations that come with a certain body of land. In faery terms, these will comprise the faes' right and expectation to be given a share of food products, to be able to use the human occupiers' homes and other buildings and (even) to have certain areas of land set aside and preserved solely for them (see later in this book). The Good Folk are a continual presence on the land – and a continual influence upon its usage and meaning.

I agree with Nash's analysis of the nature of the British spirit of place. Whether we consider the pixies of the south west, the Welsh *tylwyth teg* or the Yarthkins of East Anglia, they are all a part of the terrain in which they reside; they are the animating spirit of those moors, mountains and fens. Scottish faery authority, John Gregorson Campbell, understood this aspect of faery nature too: for example, he described the Highland *glaistig* as "acting as tutelary guardian of the site to which she is attached." She haunts castles and cattle folds and is dedicated to the welfare of those locations and their inhabitants.[7]

One thing is certain, and that is that human populations have long recognised the faeries' rights over the land and the need to respect these. The faery population requires land to cultivate and land for grazing just as much as their human neighbours and, as a result, Scottish communities long set aside a portion of their fields for them. This practice was widespread, despite Church condemnation, as is revealed by an entry in the *Book of the Universal Kirk*, recording a resolution made at a session held on May 13th 1594. This condemned:

---

7 Campbell, J.G. *Superstitions of the Highlands.* p45.

"the horrible superstitioune usit in Garioch [Aberdeenshire], and dyvers parts of the countrie, in not labouring ane parcel of ground dedicat to the devil, under the title of the *Guidman's Croft*: the Kirk, for remedy thereof, has found meit that ane article be formit to the Parliament, that ane act may proceed from the Estaites thairof, ordaining all persones, possessors of the said lands, to cause labour the samen betwixt and anecertaine day appointit thereto, otherways, in caice of disobedience, the same land to fall in the King's hands to be disponit to such persones as pleases his Majestie, who will labour the same."

That subsistence farmers should be prepared to give up much needed land to their Good Neighbours – and, as a result, needed to be forced by law to farm them – indicates the seriousness with which they took the faery presence in their lives. Their regard for, and probably dread of, the faeries is further underlined by the fact that good Christian souls would risk the wrath of the Church in order to appease supernatural beings – not demons, admittedly – but still a category of person outside the hierarchy recognised by the Bible.[8]

LIEGE & LEAF: FAIRIES AND FERTILITY

If the faes are, indeed, closely tied to the soil and the inner life of the land, they can readily be understood to work as beneficial factors in fertility. This function of promoting

---

8   Peterkin, A. *The Book of the Universal Kirk of Scotland* (1839) p402; Walter Scott, *Minstrelsy of the Scottish Borders*. Vol.2; see too my *How Things Work in Faery* (2021) pp14–15.

growth and abundance can, in fact, be seen in folklore from across Britain.

In East Anglia, the local fairies are variously called the Yarthkins, the Tiddy Ones, the Strangers or the Greencoaties. As the first name plainly shows, they are rooted in the local soil: 'Yarthkin' derives from 'earthkin' and denotes a small spirit born from the land. According to one witness interviewed in late Victorian times in the Fens, the diminutive beings are so-called because "thadoolti' th' mools" ('they dwelt in the soft earth or mould'). The Strangers act as fertility spirits, helping the growth and ripening of plant life. According to this local's account, in the spring they pinch the tree and flower buds to make them open and tug worms out of the earth; they help flowers bloom and green things grow and then, at harvest, they make the corn and fruits ripen. Without their attention, the plants would shrivel, harvest would fail and people would go hungry. In recognition of this, the Strangers receive tribute or offerings from the local people – the first share of any flowers, fruits or vegetables and the first taste of any meal or drink. If neglected, these beings may be vindictive, affecting yields, making livestock sick and even causing children to pine away.[9]

Fertility is, it would seem, a commodity or benefit that the fairies may dispense – or withhold – at their whim. An account from southern Devon underlines this starkly. A farmer living near Exmouth was on good terms with the pixies and they ensured that his farm prospered. In recognition of their aid, he provided them with an annual feast, laying out food and drink in his farmhouse and ensuring that they were undisturbed and unobserved

9 See Balfour in *Folklore*. Vol.2 (1891).

whilst they enjoyed it. Eventually the man died and his sons took over the farm. They continued his traditions, but appointed a new farm-hand who did not respect them so much. He was determined to spy on the pixies' yearly banquet, but his presence was quickly detected and the feasters vanished. From that day forth, the prosperity of the farm vanished too. The milk and cream soured, the butter would never churn and cheeses never set, the apples failed, cattle dropped dead and the crops were blighted.[10]

On the Isle of Man, the related being called the *fynoderee* has a similar relationship to the health of the land. It's said that the luck of a house resides in the sprite and, if he departs, all its happiness and prosperity will go too. Some authorities even believe that Manx agriculture as a whole has declined in parallel with the human population's waning belief in – and respect for – the *fynoderee*.[11]

The links are clear, but there is uncertainty about the exact nature of the fairies' connection to plant growth and our reliance upon them for good harvests. One theory about their origins, popular with folklorists, is that our modern fairies represent the minor fertility gods of Roman times and earlier.[12] Certainly, as the Yarthkins show, they can play a key role in fertility and, examining the British records, you soon discover that there are plentiful indications that the fairies are intricately associated with the weather and plant growth and with the fertility of not just farm livestock but of people too.

---

10 *Truman's Exeter Flying Post.* (August 18th 1869) p6 – 'Devonshire Pixies.'
11 Douglas. *Forgotten Dances.* p22; Train. *Isle of Man.* Vol.2. p138; Harrison, *Mona Miscellany.* p173; Rhys. *Manx Folklore.* Part One; *Manx Notes & Queries* (1904) p99; Gill. *Manx Scrapbook* (1929). c.4;
12 See, for example, Lewis Spence. *British Fairy Origins.*

Human Fertility

Faery researcher, Walter Evans Wentz, visiting Skye in 1910, recorded a folk tale that explicitly puts the faes in the role of the classical fates, determining the life spans of humankind. It seems best to reproduce the entire story here, which he titled, *The Fatal Peat Ember.*

"An aged nurse who had fallen fast asleep as she sat by the fire, was holding on her knees a newly-born babe. The mother, who lay in bed gazing dreamily, was astonished to see three strange little women enter the dwelling. They approached the unconscious child, and she who seemed to be their leader was on the point of lifting it off the nurse's lap, when the third exclaimed: "Oh! Let us leave this one with her as we have already taken so many!" "So be it," replied the senior of the party in a tone of displeasure, "but when that peat now burning on the hearth shall be consumed, her life will surely come to an end." Then the three little figures passed out. The good wife, recognizing them to be fairies, sprang from her bed and poured over the fire all the water she could find, and extinguished the half-burnt ember. This she wrapped carefully in a piece of cloth and deposited at the very bottom of a large chest, which afterwards she always kept locked.

Years passed, and the babe grew into a beautiful young woman. In the course of time, she was betrothed; and, according to custom, not appearing in public at church on the Sunday preceding the day appointed for her marriage, remained at home alone. To amuse herself, she began to search the contents of all the keeping-places in the house, and came at last to the chest containing the peat ember. In her haste, the good mother had that day forgotten the key of the chest, which was now in the lock. At the bottom of the chest the girl found a curious packet containing nothing but a morsel of peat, and this apparently useless thing she tossed away into the fire. When the peat was well kindled, the young girl began to feel very ill and, when her mother returned, was dying. The open chest and the blazing peat explained the cause of the calamity. The fairy's prediction was fulfilled."[13]

The Skye story indicates faery powers over mortality. In its final scene, Shakespeare's *A Midsummer Night's Dream* makes clear that the fairies influence human fertility as well. The fairies under Titania and Oberon circulate the palace after the double wedding has taken place, bringing blessings to the beds of the newly married couples:

"And the issue there create,
Ever shall be fortunate…
And the blots of Nature's hand,
Shall not in their issue stand.
Never mole, harelip or scar,
Nor mark prodigious such as are
Despised in nativity,
Shall upon their children be."

Likewise, at least as late as the close of the nineteenth century, it was believed, in parts of Scotland, that it was fairies who brought babies into the world. At Halloween, unharvested cabbages were pulled up by children and the

13 Evans-Wentz, W.Y. *The Fairy Faith in Celtic Countries*. p96.

stalks were placed on window ledges and door sills. The hope was that the souls of babies, trapped within the roots and earth, would be freed and would join each family as a new sister or brother during the forthcoming year.[14]

At the other extreme, as we have just seen, the faes can control life-spans. In between these two poles, it ought not to surprise us that they may also be interested in ensuring that offspring are properly cared for and grow well and they may therefore warn or even punish adults who neglect them.[15]

'A Spring Clean for the May Queen' – Controlling the Seasons

The intimate links existing between balance and harmony within Faery and the health of the human world are brought out explicitly in Shakespeare's *A Midsummer Night's Dream*. Early in the play, Titania describes how her quarrel with Oberon has disrupted the natural world. Strong winds have blown in thick fogs and the rivers have overflowed their banks. Crops and livestock have been blighted by both rains and frosts:

> "The ox hath therefore stretch'd his yoke in vain,
> The ploughman lost his sweat, and the green corn
> Hath rotted ere his youth attain'd a beard;
> The fold stands empty in the drowned field,
> And crows are fatted with the murrion [murrained]
>   flock…"[16]

14 Walsh. *Curiosities of Popular Customs*, p510; Shakespeare, W. *A Midsummer Night's Dream*. Act V, scene 2.

15 Addy. *Household Tales*. pp40 & 42.

16 Shakespeare, W. *A Midsummer Night's Dream*. Act II, scene 1.

Titania later summarises her influence over the weather – and hence over the yields of the crops: "I am a spirit of no common rate:/The summer still doth tend upon my state."[17]

These are vivid descriptions of the woes that can befall nature if the fairies do not lend their guiding hand and support. We know, too, from other sources, of their powers to control the climate, and shall discuss these in the next chapter.[18] Most often in accounts we find these powers wielded to punish or harm individual humans who have in some way offended or violated fairykind, but it must follow that, as well as sanctioning offences and trespasses by wrongdoers, they are able to manipulate climatic conditions in order to influence the seasons and the sprouting and ripening of crops.

Offerings for Fertility

It seems very apparent, then, that earlier generations understood that the fairies controlled every aspect of the natural world and that, as a result, they could bring either prosperity or ruin to communities as they chose. Given this power, their propitiation was fundamental to human life and health. We see instances of this from all around the British Isles. In one case, for example, a Dartmoor sheep farmer's flock was plagued by disease. He concluded that the only way of saving his stock and his livelihood was to go to the top of a tor and there sacrifice a sheep to the pixies – a move which promptly alleviated the problem.[19]

---

17 Shakespeare, W. *A Midsummer Night's Dream*. Act III, scene 1.
18 See my *Beyond Faery* (2020). cc.1 & 7, for more on this.
19 Clinton-Baddeley, V.C. *Dartmoor*. London: A & C Black (1925) p97.

Scottish folklore provides clear examples of the influence of a whole class of supernatural beings over the health and fertility of livestock. Across the Highlands, the custom was to make regular offerings of milk to *glaistigs, gruagachs, urisks* and *loireags*. These creatures have both a direct and indirect influence upon the wellbeing of farm animals. They tend the beasts in the fields, driving them to pasture and watching over them when the human herders are otherwise occupied. They ensure that the beasts are not attacked, stray into harm or trespass onto the crops where they would cause damage. More intangibly, their presence appears to be beneficial and ensures a constant supply of good quality milk. The *glaistig* of Sron-Charmaig used to check the cows' udders to ensure that the maids had milked them properly. The *gruagach* at East Bennan used to herd the community's cattle, singing to the animals as she did so. They never had accidents and, moreover, they were never stricken by disease. Offerings of milk were made to the *gruagach* and *glaistig* in recognition of the benefits they brought, but if the milk was neglected or withheld, the cows would give no milk or one might die. Urisks too will herd cattle and perform farm chores; the offerings made to the *loireag*, though, are more a matter of protection money as, in the absence of any such gifts of milk, she will simply suck it directly from the udders of cows, goats and sheep in the fields.[20]

Offerings were not confined to terrestrial sprites. At Halloween, the population of the Hebridean island of Lewis would attend a Church ceremony that included

20 Carmichael, Alexander. *Carmina Gadelica* (1900) vol.2, p306; Campbell, J.G. *Superstitions.* p163; MacDougall & Calder. *Folk Tales & Fairylore.* pp217 & 267; MacKenzie. *Scottish Folklore.* pp185 & 218; see too my *Faery* (2020) c.8 and *Beyond Faery* (2020) c.8.

pouring ale into the sea in the hope that the sprite called 'Shony' (*Seonaidh*) would guarantee a good supply of seaweed in the year ahead. The same was done on the remote isle of St Kilda, where shells, pebbles, rags, pins, nails and coins were thrown into the waves. Seaweed may not seem very important to most of us today, but it was a vital fertiliser and source of winter fodder for cattle, so a plentiful supply of 'sea ware' on the beaches was essential to survival. This is nicely demonstrated by the story of a ghillie of the MacDonald clan on the Isle of Skye who saw a *bean nighe* (a type of banshee) washing a shroud at Benbecula. He crept up and seized her, thereby earning the right to three wishes. That, of all the things he chose, one was a guarantee that the loch near his home would be full of seaweed, indicates the significance of humble kelp to the Highland economy.[21]

On the River Tweed, until around the mid-nineteenth century, salt was sprinkled on the water for the river faeries so as to guarantee a good catch of fish. This last example raises most clearly a possible alternative interpretation of these aquatic cases. Whereas the *gruagachs* and *glaistigs* visibly and directly interact with livestock to ensure their health and fecundity, the equivalent cannot be shown for most marine and riverine faeries. Possibly then, rather than promoting fertility, these latter offerings are more concerned with petitioning the spirit to agree to make plants and animals in their domain available to humans. They are, if you like, a payment to persuade the faery to release fish and seaweed for our use. Interestingly, though,

---

21 Martin, M. *A Description of the Western Isles of Scotland* (1716) p28; Dalyell, J. *The Darker Superstitions of Scotland* (1834) p545; MacCulloch. *The Misty Isle of Skye.* p243.

another story relates how the spirit of the River Tweed once slept with the local laird's wife, giving him an heir – a much more literal dispensation of fertility upon humans than we have so far considered.[22]

Summary

The faeries are, in general, symbols of natural life and growth in all its forms. Faery lore expert, Lewis Spence, noted that the worship of faery spirits – perhaps thought of as the dead or as ancestors – at ancient burial mounds (of which practice more shall be said later in chapter four) is connected directly with the idea of fertility, whether that is human, animal, cereal and/or vegetational.

> "The entire evidence of the fairy tradition is indeed eloquent of such a condition of affairs. The elves were thought of as assisting the process of human gestation and birth. The fecundity and guardianship of cattle was their peculiar care and the festivals of sowing and reaping are known to have been under their particular protection. The fairy tradition... presents a document so completely in favour of this hypothesis that one could desire no better testimony regarding its authenticity."[23]

ECO-FAIRIES?

A recent book on modern paganism and fairy belief, *Magic and Witchery in the Modern West*, suggested that many

---

22 Mackinlay, *Folklore of Scottish Lochs* (1893) p160; MacPherson. *Primitive Beliefs in North East Scotland* (1929) p67.

23 Spence. *Minor Traditions of British Mythology* (1984) p150.

of the contemporary conceptions of fairies as planetary guardians and green protectors came not from age-old faery tradition but from books like Cicely Mary Barker's flower fairy series, that adult pagans had seen and absorbed as children.[24] To what degree is this true? Is the view of faeries as green champions really so recent and untraditional a development?

As we've already begun to see, there's a reasonable amount of evidence to indicate that faeries have been connected with nature conservation and environmental causes for quite a long time. By way of immediate illustration, there is a widespread popular story of a woodcutter just about to fell a tree who is stopped by the appearance of a fairy being from beneath the ground. This is described as having happened as far apart in Britain as Northamptonshire and Nithsdale in the Scottish Borders. We shall return to this subject later, but the geographical spread of this story may imply that it is a view of Faery that's been around for some time.[25]

The 'eco-fairy' as a concept does not appear new, therefore, even if the label is. The sensibility has been present for several centuries. An examination of the folklore and literary sources discloses three interrelated functions that the faes were believed to undertake: they cared for small mammals and birds; they had a special link with certain flowers and trees and, lastly, they assumed a more general supervisory role over the natural world, keeping it in balance and preventing over-exploitation and pollution.

---

24 Feraro and White (2019).
25 Sternberg, T. *The Dialect and Folklore of Northamptonshire* (1851) p135; Wilson, W. *Folklore and Genealogies of Uppermost Nithsdale* (1904) p73.

'A Bustle in your Hedgerow' – Fairies' Furry Friends

Fairies not only live and play in the countryside: according to Victorian poetry they talk to the birds, teach them how to sing and keep their eggs warm in the nest by curling up to sleep beside them.[26]

As far back as the start of the seventeenth century, in fact, there is evidence of the fairies being seen as friends and protectors of wildlife. Sir William Browne in *Britannia's Pastorals* imagined the fairies

> "Teaching the little birds to build their nests,
> And in their singing how to keepen rests …"[27]

It seems, therefore, that the poetic and popular conceptions of the faeries' role in nature went hand in hand, for there are reported encounters with fairies helping birds find berries in the snow and looking after wildlife in wintry weather. Early Victorian child poet, Annie Isabella Brown, imagined the fairies describing how:

> "We gathered flannel-mullen leaves,
> Against the winter's cold;
> To keep the little dormouse warm,
> Within its hedgerow hold."[28]

---

26 Allingham, William. *Prince Brightkin*; Conkling, Hilda. *Fairies Again*. See also the illustration 'A rehearsal in fairy land' by Richard Doyle in which a tiny girl fairy conducts a chorus of songbirds.
27 Browne (1613) Book I.
28 Johnson, Marjorie. *Seeing Fairies*. pp72 & 135–6; Brown, Annie Isabella. 'Fairy May Day Gathering, No.2 The Sylvan Fairies' Lay,' in *Lyrical Pieces* (1869, written 1847–49).

Poet Menella Bute Smedley also imagined the fairies "twisting threads of bloom and light" to make butterflies' wings. These are highly romanticised views of Faery, but the fundamental link with the natural world, and its wellbeing and development, is key.[29]

'Mellow Yellow'? Faery Flowers

Just as there was understood to be active supernatural involvement with the animal kingdom, folk tradition identifies two aspects to the relationship between fairies and plants. They are attracted to certain herbs, whether supernaturally or for merely utilitarian reasons, such as for herbal cures or even as clothing (foxgloves, for example, are called fairy gloves and fairy thimbles). The faeries' familiarity with the healing properties of a large number of different herbs indicates their long and detailed investigations of the natural world around them.[30] Secondly, the fairies are said to inhabit certain trees, such as oaks, thorns and elders (this is examined in the following chapter).

Various flowers are linked to faes, such as periwinkle and wild thyme. Some were so closely associated with the faeries that they were even said to predispose individuals to being struck by elf-shot. These include the foxglove, cow-parsnip, dock and water lily. The latter, in Gaelic, was so intimately entwined with fae-caused disease that it was called *buaillte* ('stricken') or *rabhagach* ('warning'). Rather similar was the 'fairy grass' or 'quaking grass'. Stepping on it made the walker faint and desperately hungry. Eating a

---

29 *The Butterfly and the Fairies.*
30 See my *Faery Lifecycle* for full details of this.

piece of oat cake was felt to be the best remedy for such an affliction.

Cowslips are believed to be imbued with a faery charm that helps to discover hidden treasure – hence in some places their yellow flowers are called 'fairy keys' which will unlock secret riches (forget-me-nots have a similar power). The closely related primrose is also a fae bloom. In one story from Somerset, a little girl who had got lost in a wood when she was picking the yellow flowers accidentally touched a faery rock with the posy she'd gathered. In response the faeries appeared, gave her presents and guided her back home. An old miser heard this account and tried to repeat it. He picked a bunch of primroses too, but had the wrong number of flowers in the bunch – and was taken by the faeries and never seen again. Oddly though, on the Isle of Man, the primrose was seen as protective against the little folk, so that children would gather them on May Eve and strew them before doors to stop the faes entering.[31]

In Highland Scotland the cowslip is called the 'fairy wort' (earnaid in Gaelic). It is believed to be a powerful, magical herb which grants a lifelong protection against slanders and misfortune, if picked from a fairy knoll, as the following charm indicates:

"Pluck will I the fairy wort,
With expectation from the fairy bower,
To overcome every oppression,
As long as it be the fairy wort.

---

31 Briggs, K. & Tongue, R. *Folktales of England* (1965) pp34–35; Hull. *Folklore of the British Isles.* p253.

Fairy wort, fairy wort,
I envy the one who has thee,
There is nothing the sun encircles,
But is to her a sure victory.

Pluck will I my honoured plant,
Plucked by the great Mary, helpful mother of the
    people,
To cast off me every tale of scandal and flippancy,
Ill-life, ill-love, ill-luck,
Hatred, falsity, fraud and vexation,
Until I go in the cold grave beneath the sod."

The 'fairy bower' that is mentioned here is called *bruth* in Gaelic and denotes a faery hill or the site of an ancient broch, a class of monument that is often associated with the *sith* folk, as we shall see in chapter four. You'll notice too in this charm the combination of Christian prayer with a much older mythology.[32]

St John's wort (in Gaelic *achlusan challum chille*) is another yellow-flowered herb with a powerful reputation. It protects against faery attacks and cures the illnesses they inflict, such as cramps, stitches and itches.[33] Moreover, just like the primrose, St John's wort appears to have a dual efficacy. John Gregorson Campbell relates two stories that illustrate that the plant both attracts as well as repels the *sith*.

"A young man, named Callum, when crossing the rugged hills of *Ard-meadhonach*, in Mull, fell in with some St John's wort, a plant of magic powers, if found

---

32 Carmichael. *Carmina Gadelica*. Vol.2. pp114 & 309–310.
33 Briggs. *Fairies in Tradition & Literature*. p84.

when neither sought nor wanted. He took some of it with him. He suffered from small swellings below the toes and, on coming to a stream, sat down and bathed them in the water. Looking up, he saw an ugly little woman, who had no nostrils, sitting on the other side of the stream with her feet resting against his own. She asked him for the plant he had in his hand, but he refused to give it. She asked him to make snuff of it then and give her some. He answered, "What could she want with snuff, when she had no nostril to put it in?" He left her and went further on. As he did not come home that night, his friends and neighbours next day went in search of him. He was found by his father asleep on the side of a *cnoc* (a small hillock) and, when he was awakened, he thought, from the position of the sun, that he had only slept a few minutes. He had, in fact, slept for twenty-four hours. His dog lay sleeping in the hollow between his shoulders, and had 'neither hair nor fur' on. It is supposed it had lost the hair in chasing away the fairies and protecting its master.

In what seems to be another version of this story, a herd-boy was sitting in the evening by a stream bathing his feet. A beautiful woman appeared on the other side of the stream, and asked him to pull a plant she pointed out, and make snuff of it for her. He refused, asking what need had she of snuff, when she had no nostrils? She asked him to cross the stream, but he again refused. When he went home, his step-mother gave him his food and milk as usual. He gave the whole of it to his dog, and the dog died from the effects."[34]

34 Campbell. *Superstitions.* pp104–105.

There are numerous faery elements here: the inability to cross running water, the noticeable deformity, the effect of the *sith*-being on the dog (which we'll examine in detail later on) and the potentially fatal impact of faery interaction. The faery woman's wish to acquire the St John's wort is our focus right now. Possibly the *bean sith* is unable to pick it herself, indicating that, whilst it is still growing, it might be effective against her, but she can clearly ingest it without ill-effects once it's been picked. Various Scottish Gaelic charms indicate the plant's extensive powers. As the story from Mull indicates, St John's wort should be found by chance, not after a search, in order to retain its magic qualities, and the finder will then exclaim:

> "Saint John's wort, Saint John's wort,
> Without search, without seeking!
> Please God and Jesus Christ
> This year I shall not die."

The herb is especially prized when it's found growing inside the flock's fold, because the finder then knows they will be happy, and their sheep will be safe and plentiful, throughout the coming year. The person who discovers it says:

> "Saint John's wort, Saint John's wort,
> I envy whosoever has you,
> I will pluck you with my right hand,
> I will preserve you with my left hand,
> Whoever finds you in the cattle fold,
> Shall never be without cattle."

The Gaelic name for the wort means 'St Columba's plant', because there is a tradition that he carried the herb with him when he went preaching. It's therefore a comprehensive protection for people as well as their livestock:

"I will pick my plant,
As a prayer to my king,
To quiet the wrath of men of blood,
To check the wiles of wanton women.
I will pick my plant,
As a prayer to my king,
That mine may be its power,
Over all I see.
I will pick my plant,
As a prayer to the three,
Beneath the shade of the trinity of grace,
And of Mary, the mother of Jesus."

A further charm to be said if the plant is found brings out the St John's wort's beneficial influences:

"Plantlet of Columba,
Without seeking, without searching,
Plantlet of Columba,
Under my arm for ever!
For luck of men, for luck of means, for luck of wishes.
For luck of sheep, for luck of goats.
For luck of birds, for luck of fields,
For luck of shell-fish, for luck offish.
For luck of produce and kine,
For luck of progeny and people,
For luck of battle and victory.

On land, on sea, on ocean,
Through the three on high,
Through the three a-nigh.
Through the three eternal,
Plantlet of Columba,
I pick you now, I pick you now."[35]

Plainly these various invocations have been developed in a human, Christian society, but the benefits of finding St John's wort – to protect individuals and to bring them good fortune in all their affairs, as well as giving them power and influence over others – are obvious. These are likely to be just as desirable to faery kind as to mortals, hence the importuning demands of the two Mull banshees recounted earlier.

Broom is another yellow flower with faery associations. Poet William Browne of Tavistock described the faeries dancing in "a field of yellow broome;/Or in meadows, where/ Mints perfume the gentle aire." The ballad, *The Broomfield Wager,* or *Broomfield Hill,* describes how a knight and a lady make bets with each other whether she can go to Broomfield Hill and return still a virgin. The knight's barely concealed plan is to waylay her there and take advantage of her. The lady is advised by a 'witch' to walk nine times around the hill, after which she will find her lover asleep. She is to sprinkle him with broom flowers to make him sleep more soundly and she is then to place her brooch on his chest so that he knows, when he awakes, that she had been there and that he missed his chance. The lady does as she was instructed and the charm works.

---

35 Carmichael. *Carmina Gadelica.* Vol.2. pp97–103.

The knight is unable to wake up and molest her and she wins her bet.[36]

Flowers that are said to repel the fairies include the marsh marigold (or Mary wort), mugwort, verbena (either sewn into babies' clothes or drunk as a tea by adults) and the fruits of the sea-weed called 'sea grapes' or 'fairy eggs' (*uibhean sithein*), which are gathered, dried and worn as charms.[37]

As protectors of their environment, the faeries may treat trespasses against flowers as seriously as the felling of woodland timber. There is said to be a lake in the Brecon Beacons where access was once possible to see a 'faery garden' on an island in the middle. Once a year, on May Day, the island became visible and humans were able to visit this 'paradise' full of fruit; the resident *tylwyth teg* would give the mortals gifts of flowers and fruit and tell their fortunes. The visitors could stay as long as they liked, the only condition being that they should never take anything away with them. Sadly, one time a man picked flowers and took them home, for which violation of the faeries' rules he lost his senses and access to the island has forever afterwards been barred. It's possible that this prohibition is related to a wider feature of the *tylwyth teg* who, it is said, "have not the power to destroy a blade of grass." This being the case, much of the faery status as eco-guardians might really derive from a magical source rather than being the result of any principled objection to environmental degradation.[38]

---

36 Browne. *The Shepheardes Pipe* (1614).
37 Cameron, J. *The Gaelic Names of Plants* (1900).
38 Rhys. *Celtic Folklore*. pp21& 170; *Bye Gones*. (June 19th 1901) p25.

'A Gift from a Flower to a Garden' – Flower Fairies

As the folklore evidence hopefully shows, the associations between flowers and faeries were well established, so that, in the early twentieth century, it was a relatively easy transition from these to come up with the idea of flower fairies as popularised by artists Cicely Baker and Margaret Tarrant. This concept of child-like spirits living within – and dressing like – plants and blossoms is very a twentieth century phenomenon, but the foundations are much deeper and older. Moreover, although the flower fairies are very much a product of a growing market for illustrated books aimed at children, the tradition is concerned with fundamental issues of growth, health and reproduction.[39]

The huge commercial success of the flower fairies tends to create an impression that they were solely the invention of artists Cicely Mary Baker and Margaret Tarrant. In fact, their very memorable images are simply the culmination of an evolutionary process in popular culture. It looks as though the first step towards the flower fairy idea was an emphasis on the affinity between fairies and particular flowers. Next, it was an easy step to conceive of the spirits living in those flowers, a step that the miniaturisation of the fairies popularised by Shakespeare and his contemporaries facilitated. Inevitably, too, the fairy character began to be softened by its association with bloom, scent and colour.

This change seems to have proceeded gradually from the seventeenth century, judging by scattered indications in our literature. For instance, William Browne (1588–1643) in his verse *The Rose*, imagined that "the nimble fairies

---

39 See Spence, Lewis. *British Fairy Tradition.* pp178–80.

by the pale-faced moon/Water'd the root and kissed her pretty shade." From the eighteenth century, there is good literary evidence for the idea of fairies taking up residence in flowers. Coleridge, for example, described "Fays/ That sweetly nestle in the foxglove bells." His contemporary George Darley imagined little fairies with scented wings emerging at night from blossoms and flitting moth-like from flower to flower, enjoying nectar like wine.[40]

By the late nineteenth century, this idea was exceedingly widespread: American poet Madison Julius Cawein repeatedly housed his fays in toadstools or in blooms; and in his adult fairy tale, *Phantastes*, Scottish author George MacDonald described how "the flowers die because the fairies go away, [it is] not that the fairies disappear because the flowers die. The flowers seem a sort of house for them, or outer bodies, which they can put on and off when they please... you would see a strange resemblance, almost a oneness between the flower and the fairy... [but] whether all flowers have fairies, I cannot determine." When J. M. Barrie adopted these ideas for *Peter Pan in Kensington Gardens*, he was simply making use of an already well-established idea – although the success of his books and plays took it to a much wider audience.[41]

Consequent upon the faeries inhabiting flowers, other connections were seen- for example, gardens become an ideal place to see fairies according to the poetry of Philip Bourke Marston and others. It was also during the nineteenth century that the fairies' role as conservators of plant life was crystallised. Edwin Arnold had fairies promise to help a love-sick poet because "Thou hast never

---

40 Darley, George (1795–1846). *What the Toys do at Night* and *The Elf Toper*.
41 Peter Pan in Kensington Gardens, 1906, Chapter IV.

plucked daisy or heather bell/From the emerald braes where the fairies dwell." The fairies' floral duties are spelled out in detail in *The Wounded Daisy* by Menella Bute Smedley.[42] They are to be found at work in the corners of meadows:

> "Perhaps you'll see them…
> setting the lilies steady,
> Before they begin to grow;
> Or getting the rosebuds ready
> Before it is time to blow.
> A fairy was mending a daisy
> Which someone had torn in half…"

According to numerous nineteenth century poets, the fairies shaped and inspired growth and, even, taught the plants how to grow at special schools over the winter.[43]

Finally, Menella Bute Smedley made an important leap by involving humans as partners in the task of caring for the natural world:

> "Then pull up the weeds with a will,
> And fairies will cherish the flowers."[44]

There are, then, two conceptions of the exact inter-relationship between fairies and the natural world. The first is that they exist simply as a part of the natural world and its processes. The second, and more significant, is that

---

42 Arnold, Edwin (1832–1904). *The Fairy's Promise.*
43 Wynne, Annette. *Beginning to Grow* and *Fairy School*; Madison Cawein. *In Solitary Places* and *There are Faeries*.
44 *A Slight Confusion* in *Poems Written for a Child*, 1869.

they act as 'guardians of nature', actively watching over plants, animals and the earth as a whole, keeping the intricate systems in balance.

The flower fairies, however, whilst being iconic and memorable, are an invention. They are a fabrication of the imagination, created in the artists' studio for the purpose of delighting children in the nursery. They were designed, rather than arising from the observations and encounters preserved in tradition. They have been imposed upon nature, instead of arising organically from it. The flower faeries are attractive, but their widespread popularity should not blind us to the fact that similar ideas were in circulation before Baker and Tarrant put brush to paper.[45]

Fairies and the Green Revolution

Many contemporary writers on fairy matters stress how the faes are opposed to intensive agriculture, to the overuse of fertilisers, to pollution and to general environmental degradation. It would be easy to imagine that these ideas are wishful thinking that has been imported into the faery faith since the 1960s, but the evidence indicates that they were present to some extent in much earlier folklore and, thence it would seem, in literature, well before any conception of the harms of over-intensive cultivation even occurred to the scientific community.

We have already seen the story of the faery preventing a tree felling and the idea of fairies protecting and repairing flowers. These themes are far from unique. In the Scottish Highlands, we find traces of similar beliefs. For example,

---

45 For more on these artists, and their imitators, see my *Twentieth Century Faery Art* (2020).

Knock Hill near Largs was reputed to be full of elves, and the site of the old 'Tron Tree', which grew in the centre of the village, was a favourite gathering place for the little folk. A sow which belonged to the man who was foolish enough to cut down the Tron Tree, was found dead in its byre the morning after the felling. In another account from the same locality, a man cut a slip from an ash tree growing near a fairy dwelling. On his way home that evening, he stumbled and fell. He heard the fairies give a laugh at his mishap. Throughout that night, he was carried through the air over the countryside by the fairy host. Such was the shock and exhaustion caused by this experience that he knew nothing of what was happening to him until, in the morning, he found himself in the byre, astride a cow, and holding on to it by its horns.[46]

The idea of faeries as active defenders of the natural world was therefore accepted in folk belief from at least the start of the nineteenth century, a situation that was reflected in the literature of the time. In his poem, *Alice Brand*, Sir Walter Scott first eulogised life in the forest: "Merry it is in the good greenwood," but then had his fugitive lovers, Alice and Richard, felling trees for shelter and fires. The ringing of the axe is heard within the hill where the elfin king lives and he demands:

> "Why sounds yon stroke on the beech and oak,
> Our moonlight circle's screen,
> Or who comes here to chase the deer,
> Beloved of our Elfin Queen?"

---

46 J. G. Campbell, J.G. *Superstitions.* pp76–78.

The king then sends out a dwarf to defend his woods and game and to punish the intruders with "curse of the wither'd heart,/The curse of the sleepless eye."[47]

Fairies have always been linked more closely to rural and uncultivated locations than to towns, although it would be wrong to suggest that they're never seen in urban places (and the evidence of the recent *Fairy Census* and of the witness accounts recorded in Marjorie Johnson's *Seeing Fairies* both suggest this is changing anyway). Even in the countryside, though, they're not a people solely of wild places and woods. They often live and work around human farms (the hobs and the brownie type of spirit are the best-known examples of this) and they frequently take advantage of the human environment, using mills, barns and other agricultural structures and dancing in pastures and meadows at night. There is no antipathy with agriculture as such, therefore.

That said, ideas of fairies as a champion of more traditional, organic, self-sufficient production date back to the mid-nineteenth century at the very latest. For example, folklorist Evans-Wentz in the 1900s heard in Scotland that the Highland clearances of the crofting population to make way for sheep grazing also drove off the *sith* folk. Highlander John Dunbar of Invereen told him that "no one sees them now because every place on this parish where they used to appear has been put into sheep and deer and grouse and shooting." A vision of the faeries fighting with sheep was seen, in fact, as a premonition of what was to follow.[48]

---

47 'Alice Brand' in Sir Walter Scott's *Lady of the Lake* (1810). Canto 4.
48 Evans-Wentz, W.Y. *Fairy Faith*. p94.

Conclusion

The faeries of Britain can be conceived not just as the most ancient residents of the land, but as its soul, its animating spirit. They are not just closely identified with the landscape, they may be seen to be at the very heart of the landscape and, as such, concerned with all aspects of its development and welfare.

Works such as *Peter Pan* and the various *Flower Fairy* books unquestionably popularised the conception of the fairy as protector and champion of nature, but these ideas had been around since Elizabethan times and had been consolidating during the Victorian period. Such perceptions of the faeries are, arguably, as traditional as notions of them dancing in rings and stealing children. The 'green fairy' is not, therefore, some hippy, environmentalist creation, grafted on in recent decades, but is a fundamental element of the nature of Faery.

One final point must be made. Particularly in these times of climate emergency and ecological collapse, it is possible to overemphasise the benign qualities of the natural world in the face of those negative aspects – storms, floods and heat waves – which have been triggered by human activity. Whilst humankind has a considerable burden of blame, that is to downplay the dangerous side of nature even in its normal state.

British faery-lore recognises that nature can be cruel and that it needs to be approached with respect and caution. The best illustrations of this are the numerous water sprites, living in rivers and pools, whose reputation is wholly malign. Beings such as Peg Powler in the River Tees and Peg o'Nell in the Ribble exist solely to prey upon the unwary and unlucky, especially children. Many rivers have a spirit that expects to take a human life on a periodic basis: amongst Scottish examples are the Don, the Dee, the Till and, lastly, the Tweed, which we have discussed previously. Nature is not always kind – nor are the faeries.[49]

---

49 McPherson. *Primitive Beliefs*. p64; see too my *Beyond Faery* (2020) c.3.

CHAPTER THREE

Fairies & the Natural World

The faes have special interactions or relationships with a number of other creatures in the natural world. It is generally assumed, although there is scant evidence on this, that they can communicate with birds, mammals and insects as well as with humans.

There is a definite affinity with wildlife. The Brown Man of the Muirs is a small, swarthy being who protects stags from indiscriminate hunting along the Scottish Borders. According to one witness, he is an angry-looking dwarf with glowing eyes. The encounter in question took place near Elsdon in the Cheviot Hills, and the Brown Man scolded a young man out hunting game, saying that he regarded the youth's actions as a trespass on his land and an interference with the beasts under his care. The dwarf claimed to live on whortle-berries, apples and nuts alone – and invited the young hunter back to his home to share a meal. The man would have gone with the dwarf had his companion not called to him at that moment. The dwarf vanished at the sound of the voice and the two agreed, on reflection, that to have accompanied him would have been fatal. Nevertheless, they ignored the warning they'd received and shot more game before returning home. This failure to respect the Brown Man's wishes was believed to have led to the sickness and death within a year of the hunter who spoke to him. A second incident seems to reveal the close relationship the faes have with wild beasts. A fairy hunter encountered by two walkers at Corrieyairaick in Inverness-shire was seen to be able to walk through a herd of deer without disturbing them at all.[1]

Similar to the Brown Man is the doonie, a type of Scottish Lowland brownie who lives in the wildest parts of the countryside. She once saved the life of a man who had fallen over a cliff whilst out hunting birds and was hanging from a hazel tree above a precipice. The man was caught by the doonie, who held out her apron so that he could drop safely into it, but at the same time he was warned by her never to seek prey there again – or else doonie might not be there to rescue him. This faery obviously has a role as guardian of the natural environment, but it's likely that she was probably also acting to preserve her privacy from human intruders.[2]

The strange relationship of fairies with wildlife is further illustrated by a very curious account of the harvest customs of Westruther parish in Berwickshire, in Scotland. When harvesting began, it was held to be very bad luck to cut a coloured snail in half with the first stroke of the sickle or scythe. If this happened, the worker had to go home, saying that their blade was blunt and wouldn't cut anything further that day. The reasoning behind this custom was that the fairies danced at night in the stubble fields and, if they were surprised by the early arrival of

1 Henderson, W. *Notes on the Folklore of the Northern Counties of England and the Borders.* pp213–214; Leyden, J. *The Court of Keeldar. www. tobarandualchais.co.uk* (1969).
2 Aitken, H. *Forgotten Heritage.* p37.

the harvesters in the morning, they would hide themselves in the shells of the grey and coloured snails, which were their favourites (like grey cats, apparently); the snails made room for the faeries when they needed to conceal themselves like this. Cutting the snail, therefore, meant that a fairy would have placed a spell on the blade for the rest of that day. To express sorrow, the only option for the worker was to go home and, the next day, to work with much greater care. If they followed these rules, they would enjoy a very lucky day instead.[3]

The faeries have also been observed to have close links with certain domesticated animals. As we shall soon see, they are seen as being very affectionate and intimate with cows (from whom they get milk). They also milk goats, but their associations with these animals are even closer still: for instance, on Guernsey they may appear at night as goats with fiery eyes. In an account from Sutherland, a man resting on a faery knoll saw what he thought was a flock of goats approaching where he lay; as they got nearer, he realised that they were in fact little people dressed in many different colours.[4] In fact, the Welsh fairies are able to shapeshift into a variety of animal forms, including dogs, cats and foxes, as well as goats.[5]

John Gregorson Campbell recorded another Highland tradition:

"In Breadalbane and the Highlands of Perthshire it is said the fairies live on goat's milk. A goat was taken

---

3 Gomme, Alice. 'Collectanea: Harvest Customs,' *Folklore*. Vol.13 (1902) p178.
4 M. de Garis. *Folklore of Guernsey* (1975). p154. *www.tobarandualchais.co.uk* (July, 1960).
5 *Wrexham & Denbighshire Advertiser* (April 20th 1878) p7: 'Welsh Fairy Mythology.'

home by a man in Strathfillan, in Perthshire, to be killed. In the evening, a stranger, dressed in green, came to the door. He was asked to enter and rest himself. He said he could not, as he was in a hurry, and on his way to Dunbuck (a celebrated fairy haunt near Dunbarton), an urgent message having come for him. He said that many a day that goat had kept him in milk. He then disappeared. He could be nothing but a fairy."[6]

The man's green clothes immediately betray his supernatural nature. What's more, his almost telepathic connection with the goat and his awareness of its impending fate indicate the close link between the species.[7]

To conclude, it's only proper to observe that faery-kind are not on good terms with *all* animals. Their interactions with dogs kept by people are very frequently hostile and violent.[8] They can also become the prey of certain creatures. On Dartmoor, for example, the faeries are hunted by the foxes, whilst a Welsh account indicates that they were also antagonistic towards rooks, though whether this stemmed from the nuisance of their noise or because the birds tried to catch the little folk is unknown.[9]

'THE SEASON OF THE WITCH' – FAERIES & THE WEATHER

As described already, British faeries control the fertility of the land. It follows naturally from this that they have an

6 Campbell, J.G. *Superstitions*. p134.
7 For more on faeries and goats, see my *Faery*. (2020) c.5.
8 See my *Darker Side of Faery*. (2021).
9 See my *British Pixie* (2021); Rhys. *Celtic Folklore*. pp140–141.

influence upon the weather and, in fact, there is plentiful evidence for this, on both a local and regional scale.

Sensitivity to climate and the time of year is a fundamental faery trait. It may be an overlooked fact, but the faes are a distinctly seasonal race. May Day is widely regarded as the start of their year, when they first appear in the mortal world and begin to dance outside again. They are thereafter present in the fields and woods until the end of October when, with Halloween, their last 'rade' or processional ride takes place. The fact that the faeries are, by and large, absent from the earth during winter highlights how closely they are tied to the cycle of growth. Very probably for this reason too, green is widely recognised as being the quintessential faery colour. Their life and activity waxes and wanes with that of nature and with the seasons.

The links of faes to the weather are longstanding, but their exact nature and meaning are not always immediately clear. For example, it is recorded that in South Wales the belief is that:

> "Friday is the faeries' day, when they have special command over the weather; and it is their whim to make the weather on Friday differ from that of other days of the week. [Thus, it is said that] 'When the rest of the week is fair, Friday is apt to be rainy or cloudy; and when the weather is foul, Friday is apt to be more fair.'"[10]

A similar obscure interconnection exists too in Scotland. In the north-east, it is said that when it rained it was a sign

---

10 Sikes. *British Goblins*. p268.

that the local faeries were baking. In another manifestation of the same idea, if the sun shone through a rain shower, children would declare that "the fairies are baking – the rain waters the bannocks." A further rendering of the association is found in a popular rhyme recorded by John Gregorson Campbell: "Rain and sun: the little people are at their meat [food or meal]." He also noted the belief that, when the wind and rain come from opposite directions, by throwing some horse droppings against the wind, the fairies can be brought down in a shower.[11]

A direct control over changes in climatic conditions and over the transitions between seasons is seen in several so-called 'hags' of the north and west of Britain. The *cailleach bheur* is a wild giant hag of the Scottish Highlands. She has a blue face and a vicious temper, in consequence of which she's also called the 'winter hag' or the 'hag of the ridges.' The *cailleach* is linked with the changing of the seasons, from winter to summer and back. She is particularly associated with the windy, freezing weather of early April, when she is believed to wander the hills, delaying the return of spring. She can send terrible storms, called '*cailleach* weather' or 'wolf-storms.' Finally, of course, the sun will defeat her and she will disappear in a rage until the next winter.[12]

On the Isle of Man, the *caillagh y grommagh,* 'the old woman of the gloom,' is also linked to the changing of the seasons. She appears annually on the morning of February 12th, trying to gather sufficient firewood to warm herself.

---

11 Gregor. *Notes on the Folklore.* p65; *Bye Gones.* (May 5th 1897) p106; Campbell. *Superstitions.* p26.

12 Carmichael. *Carmina Gadelica.* Vol.2, p236; Dalyell. *Darker Superstitions* p542; K. Grant, *Myth, Tradition & Story from Western Argyll.* Oban: Oban Times Press (1925). c.2; Mackenzie, *Scottish Folklore.* c.7.

If she can find enough dry sticks for a blaze, the spring will be wet. If, however, the morning is damp and she can't make a fire, the spring will be dry.[13] In the Firth of Cromarty, the weather is under the control of another blue-faced hag called Gentle Annie or Annis. She is known for her highly changeable nature: a day that starts fine and calm may end with violent storms, imperilling craft that have been tempted to put out to sea.

Akin in their behaviour to these hags are the mermaids, who can raise storms when they wish. An example of this power comes from mid-Wales. The story of Nefyn concerns a mermaid who entered into a relationship with a human male and had a sizeable family with him.

> "Once they went out in a boat for pleasure, as was their wont, with six or seven of the children accompanying them, and when they were far from the land a great storm arose; besides the usual accompaniments of a storm at sea, most unearthly screeches and noises were heard, which frightened the children and made their mother look uncomfortable; but presently she bent her head over the side of the boat, and whispered something they did not catch: to their surprise the sea was instantly calm. They got home comfortably, but the elder children were puzzled greatly by their mother's influence over the sea ..."[14]

Additionally, it appears that the death of merfolk can precipitate storms: for instance, it's said that if a selkie is shot in the sea, a storm will arise as soon as its blood

---

13 *Yn Lioar Manninagh.* Vol.1. p223.
14 Rhys. *Celtic Folklore.* p119.

mixes with the water. In other cases, the bad weather seems to be an instant environmental response to the death. The merfolk are also very sensitive to changes in the weather and the approach of storms. Fishermen believe that simply seeing a mermaid indicates that bad weather is approaching; some seafarers even believe that spotting a mermaid means that their voyage is doomed entirely. If they wish, though, mermaids can choose to warn favoured mortals of impending wind and waves.[15]

Very frequently, it appears that the faeries generate mists and fogs for concealment, as with the faery woman of the Maiden Well in the Ochil Hills or, more generally, as with the *gwrach y rhybin*, the 'hag of the mist' of the Welsh mountains, and the 'Woman of Mist' who lived on Bicknoller Hill in the western Quantock Hills. John Gregorson Campbell felt that, in the case of the *sith* of the Highlands, "a favourite time for their encounters with men seems to be the dusk and wild stormy nights of mist and driving rain, when the streams are swollen and 'the roar of the torrent is heard on the hill.'"[16]

In the cases just described, the change in the weather is a result of faery magic and is part and parcel of their other purposes – which tend to be either the abduction or misleading of people. In the ballad *Hynd Etin,* for example, the hero is said to have "coosten a mist before them all/ And away the lady has taken." Bad weather is a cover for bad faery behaviour.

---

15 *Royal Cornwall Gazette* (Aug 17th 1899) p6: 'Cornish Giants & Mermaids;' for more detail see my *Beyond Faery.* (2020) c.1.
16 Fraser. "Northern Folklore: Wells & Springs." *Celtic Magazine.* Vol.3 (1878), p31; Tongue. *Somerset Folklore*, p120; Campbell. *Superstitions.* p21; see too my *Beyond Faery.* (2020) c.7.

In other cases, mist and cloud may be as much about concealment from humans as against being a means of kidnapping humans. The Welsh faeries are only seen when the weather is a little misty: they prefer days when visibility on the mountains is poor, when a fine drizzly rain called *gwithlaw* covers the land. It's not clear to what extent the *tylwyth teg* are responsible for these conditions, but it is known that such murky days are the best times to encounter them. A shepherd living beside Llyn y Gader became infatuated with a beautiful faery woman whom he'd first met on just such a misty day and a maid living at Cwmglas near Llanberis used to leave a jugful of fresh milk and a clean towel for the *tylwyth teg* on dark and misty mornings, receiving money in return. Nonetheless, children were warned that it was on such days that people were most likely to be abducted and carried through the air by the faes, so doubtless the respective parents must have been very alarmed when some children in Denbighshire in the 1880s reported how they had watched a crowd of diminutive people dressed in blue, who ran in and out of the clouds wreathing the top of a local hill.[17]

The pixies of the south west of England, who are frequently encountered on upland moorland areas like Dartmoor, Bodmin Moor and the hills of Penwith, regularly use fog to 'pixie-lead' individuals; there are numerous examples recorded of them manipulating local weather to get victims lost, scared and confused.[18] This may be done for reasons of pure mischief or it may have a moral and corrective purpose. For instance, a man from Bishop's

17 Rhys. *Celtic Folklore*. pp33, 36, 91, 220, 223 & 228; Owen. 'Rambles Over the Denbighshire Hills,' *Archaeologia Cambrensis*. Vol.3, 5th series, no.9 (1886). p72; Owen. *Welsh Folklore*. p100.
18 See examples in my *British Pixies*.

Lydeard in the Quantock Hills came across a faery grind stone and decided to keep it as a curiosity. The pixies were angered by his presumptuous theft and wanted to punish him, so a mist promptly came down and he was led through brambles all night. Nonetheless, manipulation of the weather also seems to be used to add to the menace of offended faeries. When a man went digging for buried gold in the hillfort on Trencrom Hill, near St Ives, he first saw the sky darken, heard the wind begin to roar and then, on looking up at the flashing lightning of the looming storm, saw that hundreds of spriggans were advancing upon him to chase him away from his excavations. The combined fear of being in a storm on a hilltop and being pursued by a horde of angry elves was sufficient to make him quit in haste.[19]

Their varied motivations notwithstanding, it will nevertheless be clear that the faeries can influence climatic conditions at their will.

'I SING TO YOU OF NORTHERN LIGHTS'

The faeries can shape the weather; higher in the heavens still, they are thought to be responsible for the Northern Lights, the aurora borealis. The lights go by various names across Britain, such as the Perry Dancers in East Anglia and the Merry Dancers or *Fir Chlis* (Nimble Men) in Scotland. Their origins and faery connections also have several explanations.[20]

---

19 Tongue. *Somerset Folklore*. p114; Hunt. *Popular Romances*. Vol.2, p245 & Vol.1, p48.
20 Ritson, J. *A Dissertation on Fairies* (1831) p7; Briggs, K. *Dictionary of Fairies*. pp177 & 325; Spence. *Fairy Tradition in Britain*. p58; for the Blue Men, see my *Beyond Faery*. (2020) c.1.

According to one story (very obviously shaped by Christian beliefs), after the revolt of Satan the angels were cast out of heaven. Some fell to earth and became faeries; some fell into the sea and became the so-called *Fir Gorm,* the Blue Men of the Western Isles of Scotland; others fell only as far as the sky and are seen as the 'Northern Streamers.'[21]

Although the Merry Dancers are distinguished from the *sluagh,* who are notorious for hunting and abducting humans, theirs is still a violent existence. They are said to fight an everlasting battle, which we witness as the lights in the sky. The blood shed during this conflict gathers at first as in a red cloud below the aurora, 'the pool of blood,' before falling to earth, where it can be seen congealed as 'blood stones' called *fuil siochaire* or elves' blood in the Hebrides. The fighting of the faery hosts at Halloween likewise leaves behind traces of blood, a red liquid that seeps from lichens after frost. In some accounts, the fighting takes place between different clans of the *Fir Chlis* for possession of a faery woman.[22]

On Shetland, the lights were once feared and were called the Fighting Lasses. Now their reputation seems to have ameliorated; they are referred to as the Pretty Dancers because, on still nights, you can hear the swish of their dresses as they glide about the sky. There is even a dance tune, perhaps learned from the faeries, called the Pretty Dancers' Reel. William Allingham's poem, *The Fairies,* reflects this more benign view, describing how the faes will go "up with music on cold starry nights/To feast with the queen of the gay Northern Lights."[23]

21 Campbell. *Superstitions.* pp199–200; MacGregor. *Peat Fire Flame.* p121;
22 MacKenzie. *Scottish Folklore & Folk Life.* p222.
23 Saxby, J. *Shetland Traditional Lore.* (1932) pp189–190.

SHAPESHIFTING FAYS

The exact relationship of faeries to wild and domesticated animals is somewhat complicated and obscured by the faes' ability to assume the shape of birds and beasts. In 1584, in his horror novella, *Beware the Cat,* William Baldwin wrote what's probably our first clear statement of the fairies' shapeshifting habits:

> "I have read that ... the ayry spirits which wee call Demones, of which kinde are Incubus and Succubus, Robin Good Fellow the Fairy and Goblins, which the Miners call Telchines, could at their pleasure take upon them any other sortes."

Robin Goodfellow is our particular interest here. Also called Puck, this hobgoblin is the consummate master of transformation, as immortalised in a scene in *A Midsummer Night's Dream,* in which Puck famously boasts to a fairy about his pranks:

> "When I a fat and bean-fed horse beguile,
> Neighing in likeness of a filly foal:
> And sometime lurk I in a gossip's bowl,
> In the very likeness of a roasted crab [apple]..."[24]

All Shakespeare does here is give immortal form to the traditional character of Puck. Two other texts written about the same time give other examples of his tricks – these are *The Life of Robin Goodfellow, His Mad Pranks and Merry Jests* (1628) and a poem called *The Pranks of Puck*

---

24 Shakespeare, W. *A Midsummer Night's Dream.* Act II, Scene 1.

that has been attributed to Ben Jonson. In these works, Robin is endowed with his shapeshifting power by his fairy father Oberon, who tells him:

> "Thou hast the power to change thy shape
> To horse, to hog, to dog, to ape.
> Transformed thus, by any meanes,
> See none thou harm'st but knaves and queanes."

In the course of the stories, Puck dispenses rough justice and has simple slapstick fun in a huge variety of forms. He can, for example, transform himself into livestock such as a horse, a dog and an ox; into wild animals, including a fox, a hare, a bear and a frog; into various birds, including a crow, an owl and a raven, into other spirits such as the will of the wisp and a ghost; and, lastly, into a variety of people, including a cripple, a soldier, a young maid and fiddler.

This shapeshifting ability was by no means limited to Puck. Thus, the Puritan Henry More, writing in 1647, described "aerial devils" (who might be faeries, or sylphs, or some other kind of spirit) who could change into new forms and change back with ease, being one moment a man, another a comely maid, then a snarling dog, a bristled boar or – even – a jug of milk.[25] Needless to say, the power to transform was not limited solely to English sprites either. There is a curious story from Lochranza on Arran in which the fairy queen is seen in a most unflattering guise. A woman who was a midwife was in a field cutting oats at harvest when she saw a large yellow frog that was obviously pregnant. Another of the reapers

---

25 More, *The Prae-existence of the Soul*. Stanzas 40 & 41.

wanted to kill the creature, but the midwife felt pity for its state and remarked that it would soon benefit from the help of a woman with her skills. A little while later, she was taken at night to a nearby faery knoll to attend to the very same faery woman, now in her proper form.[26]

Fairies as Birds

In the folklore record, there are two brief mentions of British fays who can transform themselves to birds. One particular significance of this transmutation is that these fairies' wings are acquired by taking on a new bodily shape, as they evidently don't normally possess them...

The *hyter sprite*, an obscure fairy of East Anglia, is able to appear in the shape of a sand-martin and, from the Cornish story of *The Fairy Dwelling on Silena Moor*, we learn that pixy abductee Grace Hutchens is more reconciled to her captivity by the fact that she can transform into a small bird and fly near to her former lover, Mr Noy. There's a catch to the Cornish pixies' ability to transform, though. They can only change into birds and it seems each transformation shrinks the sprite so that eventually they dwindle away to virtually nothing.

Additionally, on the Isle of Man there was once a *lhiannan-shee* or fairy woman who obsessed many human men with her beauty, but then led them all into the sea, raising the waves and drowning them. Eventually the people grew tired of her depredations and they banded together and attacked her. She was only able to escape by taking on the form of a wren. This saved her, but she was thereafter cursed to appear as the tiny bird every

---

26 MacDougall & Calder. *Folk Tales & Folklore.* p271.

St Stephen's Day (December 26th), on which date the islanders would go out to hunt her between sunrise and sunset. Once again, animal shape has advantages and severe downsides, too, for the fairy adopting it.[27]

Other Faery Forms

Most faeries may take on alternative forms as a means of disguise, often to trick humans, and these are temporary transformations that hide but do not in any way replace their fundamental humanoid appearance. There are, though, faery beings who seem to alternate between a couple of forms, one of these being their predominant or 'true' appearance. We are very familiar with the mermaid, selkie and roane who can remove their fish or seal skin to reveal a human form within. I wish to add two new examples to this list.

The first comes from Wales. A young man was coracle fishing on the Towy River when he caught a large salmon. When he hauled it into his boat, the fish turned into a beautiful young woman; she tried to escape and he threatened to knock her on the head and kill her (just as he would the fish) if she didn't calm down. She retorted that she'd drown him first. A stand-off ensued, so the salmon maiden proposed that they become lovers; the youth refused this (surprisingly, perhaps) but she tried to pull him down to the *gwaelod yr afon,* the land beneath the river. This attempted drowning was repeated several times until he finally agreed to her offer. He then cut the fishing hook from her lip, after which she promptly kissed

---

27 Walsh. *Curiosities of Local Customs.* p1008.

him. Her blood on his face worked as a charm to make him hers forever. What's more, all their children had a scar on their upper lips just like their mother.[28]

It isn't clear at all from this account whether the girl spent most of her time in salmon form or whether it was just a convenient way of getting around quickly in the river. In a second account of a fish maiden from the Isle of Man, it seems as though human shape is a definite 'second best'. A fishmonger is given a salmon by a mysterious stranger, who doesn't seek money for it but insists that it must be sold whole. Because of this condition, no customers want the large fish and it remains on the shop slab when closing time comes. However, during the night the man finds the fish's skin shed and empty, but then whole again in the morning. The next night, he awakes to find a silver haired girl in his room. She is one of the daughters of the King of Salmon River who can "be fish or humans at will." The fishmonger agrees to set her free, because she cannot live for long on land. A necessary preliminary to this is to remove the hook from her mouth, which will restore her life as a salmon. In return for his kindness, he is granted a wish. This latter salmon maid appears to be, to all intents and purposes, an inland water selkie or mermaid.[29]

FAERIES & BIRDS

Faeries have several connections with birds. They may temporarily assume avian form, in addition to which, they are frequently compared to birds because of their size or

28 *Reports & Transactions of the Cardiff Naturalists Society*, vol.36, 1903, 58 – 'Some Folklore of South Wales.'

29 D. Broome, *More Fairy Tales from the Isle of Man*, 1970, 52–59.

their motion. Over and above this, there are also birds that are closely associated with the faery world.

The comparisons of fairies to flocks of small winged creatures are extremely common; in the bulk of cases, they are likened to birds rather than insects. The faery Roodmassrade was seen once in Galloway. The faeries were riding diminutive white horses, but were said to have passed over a corn field "like sparrows." Obviously, they didn't resemble birds, but the comparison is indicative of their number and their lightness: the crop in the fields was inspected the next day and it was found that not a blade had been damaged. A second Scottish witness described the *sluagh* travelling "in great clouds, up and down the face of the world like starlings." More often, it is the sound the fairies make that draws the comparison to birds. A man at Benbecula in the Hebrides heard the *sluagh* go overhead – and it sounded to him 'like a flock of plovers.' A man living near Harrogate once got up early to hoe his turnips. When he reached his field, he was astonished to discover that every row was being hoed by a host of tiny men in green. As soon as he tried to climb over the stile into the field, they fled like a flock of partridges. In another Yorkshire report from Ilkley, fairies surprised whilst bathing in the spa there made a noise "not unlike a disturbed nest of young partridges" when disturbed by the caretaker.[30]

Faery Birds

In Wirt Sikes' *British Goblins,* you will find the story of Shon ap Shenkin:

---

30 Maxwell Wood, J. *Witchcraft & Superstitious Record.* p177; Carmichael. *Carmina Gadelica.* Vol.2, p330; Pennant, T. *Tour of Scotland.* Vol.1. p110.

"Shon ap Shenkin was a young man who lived hard by Pant Shon Shenkin [in Carmarthenshire]. As he was going afield early one fine summer's morning, he heard a little bird singing, in a most enchanting strain, on a tree close by his path. Allured by the melody, he sat down under the tree until the music ceased, when he arose and looked about him. What was his surprise at observing that the tree, which was green and full of life when he sat down, was now withered and barkless! Filled with astonishment, he returned to the farm-house which he had left, as he supposed, a few minutes before; but it also was changed, grown older, and covered with ivy. In the doorway stood an old man whom he had never before seen; he at once asked the old man what he wanted there. 'What do I want here?' ejaculated the old man, reddening angrily; 'that's a pretty question! Who are you that dare to insult me in my own house?' 'In your own house? How is this? Where's my father and mother, whom I left here a few minutes since, whilst I have been listening to the charming music under yon tree, which, when I rose, was withered and leafless?' 'Under the tree! Music! What's your name?' 'Shon ap Shenkin.' 'Alas, poor Shon, and is this indeed you!' cried the old man. 'I often heard my grandfather, your father, speak of you, and long did he bewail your absence. Fruitless inquiries were made for you; but old Catti Maddock of Brechfa said you were under the power of the fairies, and would not be released until the last sap of that sycamore tree would be dried up. Embrace me, my dear uncle, for you are my uncle – embrace your nephew.' With this the old man extended his arms, but before the two men could embrace, poor Shon ap Shenkin crumbled into dust on the doorstep."[31]

In several respects, this is a typical story about the differential passage of time in Faery and the mortal risks faced by a human returning home. Such accounts date back to that of King Herla in the Middle Ages. Of course, Shon is not aware of any journey to Faery at all; he simply sat in the shade by the roadside, but somehow was transported from this world.

However, what interests me in the tale are two of the details – the tree and the bird. The tree is said to be a sycamore, which is unusual; it would not have surprised me to learn that it was a hawthorn (or perhaps an elder). As we'll see later, these are notorious fairy trees with which the Good Folk and their magic have always been closely associated; sycamores, though, don't seem to have any of these traditional associations.

The other significant feature of Shon ap Shenkin's story is the bird. It plays a key role in his abduction, and demonstrates that birds and faeries may have unsuspected links. Sadly, there are now only a few scraps of evidence of this association to be found in the folklore record of England and Wales.

Reasonably substantial is the Oxfordshire story of True John and Greedy Jack, a tale that pits a man favoured by the fairies against his jealous neighbour. Both farmers had apple trees, but John's produced abundant fruit and were always full of crowds of small green birds whilst, at night, small lights were seen in the branches, accompanied by singing and perfume. Jack was envious and one day tried

31 Sikes. *British Goblins.* pp92–94.

shooting at the trees with a shotgun to scare off the birds and damage the fruit. Instead, it was his own fruit that were peppered with shot whilst the birds pecked at his face. After this, Jack lost all his luck. When John died, Jack cut down the bounteous trees he envied so much, hoping thereby to drive the birds to live in his own, but instead a mighty wind arose and flattened his orchard. Neither the birds nor the lights were seen again. Both for their colour and for their close association to the lights, these are very obviously faery birds, a fact that probably should have been clear to Jack. From that, it should have been clear in turn that he could not force the fairies into favouring him over his rival. His downfall followed inexorably. The protective role of faeries towards apple trees is something I shall return to at the end of this chapter.

Lastly, as Wirt Sikes also recorded, there is an ancient Welsh legend of the Birds of Rhiannon (*Adar Rhiannon*). Rhiannon is one of the goddesses or fairy women of Welsh myth. Her birds' song can "wake the dead and lull the living to sleep." In a clear sign of their magical or faery nature, the birds can be remote but still sound as if they are very near. This legend appears in the *Mabinogion* in the story of Branwen, Daughter of Llyr (*Branwen ferch Llŷr*). Only seven men survived from a large force of warriors that had followed King Bran across the sea to fight the Irish. Bran himself had died of his wounds, but had commanded the survivors to cut off his head and bury it under Tower Hill in London. On their way there, the men paused at Harlech in North Wales to rest and feast. Three birds came and began singing to them so sweetly that all the songs they had ever heard before seemed unpleasant in comparison.

The feast and birdsong were so enchanting, they remained listening for seven years.[32]

The sweetness of birdsong and the dislocation of time (for a period of years to a number of men of considerable magical significance) are found in this early Welsh myth just as in the later Welsh story of Sion ap Shenkin. It seems clear from these rather fragmentary and scattered remnants that there was once a much completer knowledge of the nature and powers of faery birds, something that we have sadly lost with the passage of the years. To these scraps we may add that Evans Wentz' mention of Breton fairies who take the form of ducks, swans and magpies (an especially significant bird in British folklore) and the belief in Ireland that fairies and some of the goddesses of the *Tuatha de Danaan* appear as crows.[33]

Scottish Faery Birds

There are, in Scottish fairy tradition, some fascinating but scattered clues that offer us additional perspectives upon relationship between the Scots elves and birds.

There are a few Scottish Gaelic prayers in which the saints Mary and Brigit are described as a fairy swan and a fairy duck of peace (*Mhoire na sith* and *lacha shith* respectively). Possibly these unique and puzzling images combine some sense of lightness, softness and a magical quality. That said, the teal duck (*lacha sith*) is believed to be a herald of storms and, in this role, is very plainly lacking in any benign qualities.[34]

---

32 See Sikes. *British Goblins*. p2; and Evans Wentz. *Fairy Faith*. pp329 & 334.
33 *Fairy Faith*. pp200 & 305–7.
34 Carmichael. *Carmina Gadelica*. Vol.3. p269 & Vol.1. p317; Mackenzie. *Scottish Folklore*. p204.

Most fascinating is the Scottish folklore relating to the cuckoo. The earliest clue to the existence of a unique tradition comes from a verse romance of the early fifteenth century, *King Berdok*. The eponymous hero of the story is the ruler of Babylon, who for seven years woos a maid called Mayiola or Mayok, daughter of the King of Faery. He affectionately calls her his "golk of Maryland." A golk is a cuckoo; this particular specimen is said to be but three years old and to have but one eye – nevertheless, "King Berdok luvit her weill."

The exact date of *Berdok* is uncertain, but it was known by poet William Dunbar (1460–1522), who referred to it in his own poem, *In Secreit Place This Hyndir Nicht*, in which another lover refers to his amour as "my golk of Marie land."

These verses give us two curious problems: what's the link between cuckoos and fairies and what and where is Mary-land? The latter question is the easier of the two to resolve. The place name also appears as Mirry, May, Maiden and Murray-land. For example, in 1596, Thomas Leys of Aberdeen (along with much of the rest of his family, in fact) was accused of witchcraft and of dancing around the market cross in the town with the devil. His former girlfriend, Elspet Keid, turned against him and gave evidence that led to his execution. Thomas had told his erstwhile lover that he would take her to Murrayland and there marry her – "a man at the foot of a certain mountain being sure to rise at his bidding, and supply them with all they wanted." Given this association with supernatural powers, it seems very likely that Thomas is talking about a Faery under a hill here, although we must recognise the fact that in Scotland at the time, Murrayland was a real place too – the territory of Clan Murray.[35]

Secondly, there is a Scots ballad, "The rain rins down through Mirry-land toune." This tells the story of a young man, Sir Hew, who is killed and butchered and thrown in a well by a woman. His mother searches for him and his ghost tells her to fetch a winding sheet, whereupon:

> "And at the back of Mirry-land toune,
> It's there we twa shall meet."

Given the established links between faery and the dead, it seems reasonable to assume that the town in question has some supernatural nature.

If, as the evidence seems to indicate, Mirryland is another name for Faery – which is more usually referred to as Elphame in Scots – where exactly does this odd name derive from? It doesn't seem to have anything to do with the Virgin Mary, although in the Catholic Middle Ages her presence in people's minds is very likely to have affected the pronunciation. Rather, the root appears to be a great deal older. The word seems to descend from the Anglo-Saxon *maere,* a word that is preserved in modern English as 'nightmare' and which was glossed as 'satyr' in one Old English source. In light of this, 'goblin land' or even 'nightmare land' might be the most reasonable translation. The word clearly denotes some supernatural being – a sprite or incubus – from which it is an easy step to 'fairy' and thence 'fairyland.'[36]

---

35 Goodacre, J. 'Boundaries of the Fairy Realm in Scotland' in *Airy Nothings – Imagining the Other World of Faerie from the Middle Ages.*
36 Spence. *British Fairy Origins.* p46.

If Mirryland is fairyland, why is it particularly linked with the cuckoo? This is trickier: in Northern Europe the cuckoo is a bird associated with summer, certainly, being its best-known harbinger. In the story, *The Cuckoo and the Merry Tree,* by Frances Browne (1857), the merry tree is some sort of evergreen-like laurel, growing at the world's end, and the cuckoo brings leaves from it in spring.

However, in Scottish Gaelic tradition, the cuckoo was called *eun-sith,* the fairy bird. As just noted, there were several fairy types of birds but the cuckoo was 'the fairy bird.' It appears that the reason for this name was a belief that, instead of migrating over the winter, the bird instead hibernated underground (just like the *sith* folk themselves). For that matter, as well as migrating birds, it was the Highland belief that all seasonal flowers and plants disappeared beneath the fairy knolls to shelter during the winter months. This extended subterranean habitation led, it seems, to the cuckoo's fairy link. Equally, in the Highlands it used to be said that, if it rained when the sun also shone, either the *sith* folk were baking or a *gowk* was going to heaven. I have also read that the cuckoo was regarded as being sacred to the fairies, but I haven't been able to authenticate this.[37]

Nonetheless, there is plenty of other folklore tradition concerning the bird – for instance, it's said that, on hearing the first cuckoo in spring, you must run three times in a circle sun-wise to ensure good luck for the rest of the year. In addition, it's said that if you hear a cuckoo on April 14th, you should immediately turn over any coins that you have

37 Forbes, A.R. *Gaelic Names of Beasts* (1905) p260; Mackay, J.G. *Scottish Gaelic Studies.* Vol.3 (1929) p19; *Celtic Monthly.* Vol.1. (1892) p149; Campbell. *Superstitions.* p5; Mackenzie. *Scottish Folklore.* p204.

in your pocket. Readers will spot the fairy congruences here: the circling sun-wise and the 'turning' of an item to dispel supernatural bad luck. These practices may, of course, just be examples of more general folk magic but even so, they serve to confirm the 'uncanny' nature of the cuckoo.

FAERY HERDS

The fairies keep their own cattle, often called the *crodh sith* in the Highlands, and the faes' relationship with these beasts is very different to that usually seen with human livestock. The fairy cow is dun (*odhar*), and is 'hummel', or hornless. On Skye, however, fairy cattle are said to be speckled and red (*crodh breach ruadh*), and they are not able to cross the sea as others are reputed to do. Only a few areas of grazing land are preferred by them. When the cattle come home at night from the pasture, the following are the words used by the fairy women, standing on Dun Ghearra-seadar, near Portree, as she counts in her charge:

> "Crooked one, dun one,
> Little wing grizzled,
> Black cow, white cow,
> Little bull black-head,
> My milch kine have come home,
> O dear! that the herdsman would come!"

This verse indicates the close relationship between faery herder and beast. They seem to be able to communicate and to understand each other. This closeness no doubt explains why the *gruagach* and the *glaistig* have the reputation of being such devoted and effective cattle herders.[38]

We see exactly the same intimate links with the faery lake women, the *gwragedd annwn*, in Wales. There are numerous stories of these women being wooed and wed by human males. When the couple marries, the faery wife will bring with her a dowry of goats, horses and cattle, instantly enriching her human husband.[39]

These marriages are always subject to strict taboos, however. Frequently, the faery bride's true name will be kept from her spouse; always, he will be warned never to strike her or to allow iron to touch her. These conditions are always breached, too, sooner or later. When this happens, the wife will instantly depart, calling to her cattle (called the *gwartheg y llyn)* to follow her. The faery woman of Llyn y Fan Fach rounded up her dowry with these words:

"*Mu wlfrech, Moelfrech,*
Mu olfrech, Gwynfrech,
Pedair cae tonn-frech,
Yr hen wynebwen,
A'r las Geigen,
Gyda'r Tarw Gwyn
O lys y Brenin;
A'rllo du bach,
Sydd ar y bach,
Dere dithau, yn iach adre!"

"Brindled cow, white speckled,
Spotted cow, bold freckled,

---

38 Campbell. *Superstitions*. pp29–30.
39 Rhys. *Celtic Folklore*. Vol.1. p8.

The four field-sward mottled,
The old white-faced,
And the grey Geingen,
With the white bull,
From the court of the king;
And the little black calf
Though suspended on the hook,
Come you too, safe and sound home!"

The beasts all immediately obeyed the summons of their mistress. The 'little black calf', although it had been slaughtered, came back to life and walked off with the rest of the herd at the wife's command. As this happened in the spring, there were four oxen ploughing in one of the fields at the time; to these she cried:

"Pedwar eidion glas
Sydd ar y maes,
Denwch chwithan
Yn iach adre!"

"The four grey oxen,
That are on the field,
Come you also
Safe and sound home!"

Rhys concluded: "The whole of the farm's livestock went with the wife across towards the lake from whence they came, where they disappeared beneath its waters, leaving no trace behind except a well-marked furrow, which was made by the plough the oxen drew after them, and which remains to this day as a testimony to the truth of this story."[40]

Similar events occurred at Rhondda Fechan and Llanwynno. In a few cases, all was not entirely lost for the mortal farmer, as his cattle might have interbred with the faery beasts – so that not all his livestock departed. Equally, in another instance at Corwrion, the departed faery mother later endowed her son on his marriage with a small herd of milk cows and a bull.[41]

Sometimes the faery cattle emerged from the lake of their own accord to mingle and mate with human herds. Whilst not subject to the immediate oversight of a faery woman who brought them as a dowry, they were still subject to the care of the *tylwyth teg*. Hence, in the well-known story of the *fuwch gyfeiliorn* (the stray cow) and the farmer of Dyssyrnant in Gwynedd, when after many years the man decided to slaughter the faery cow, it provoked a woman in green to appear suddenly and to call the beasts home in a voice 'as loud as thunder.' The original cow – and all her offspring to the fourth generation – departed from the farm and disappeared into Llyn Barfog. In a related tale from Hafod y Garreg, on the shores of Llyn Arennig, a faery piper suddenly appeared one day and called the herd to follow him, in this case for no apparent reason.[42]

From the Scottish Highland comes a story very closely comparable to that recorded at Dyssyrnant. A farmer's herd had benefitted from the fact that one of the cows had annually wandered off to an island in a nearby river where she seems to have interbred with a local water-bull

---

40 Rhys. *Celtic Folklore*. Vol.1. p10.
41 Rhys. *Celtic Folklore*. pp23–24, 25, 51–52, 55 & 61.
42 Rhys. *Celtic Folklore*. pp144–145 & 149.

(*tarbh uisge*). The offspring of these unions were found to be "docile, strong and useful" and the man had prospered. After several years, though, he suggested to his family that the November cull of livestock should include the heifer who was mother of all the hybrid cattle. She had worked well and supplied plentiful milk and calves, but she was old and past her best. The words were scarcely uttered when the cow, who was stabled in the byre in the other half of the house, walked out through the side of the building as if it was paper, lowed to gather her calves together, and then led them all to the river where they disappeared, presumably joining their father.[43]

Although generally regarded as valuable assets, these faery cattle can still cause a nuisance to humans' herds. When one of them appears among a herd of cattle, the whole fold of them grows frantic, and follows the *crodh sith,* lowing wildly. The strange animal then disappears by entering a rock or knoll, and the others, unless intercepted, will follow it and will never be seen again.

FAERY DEER

As was mentioned earlier, faeries don't only get milk from cattle. They also have wild goats but in the Highlands of Scotland, most particularly, they are well-known for keeping herds of deer for milking. In some districts, such as Lochaber and Mull, deer are said to be the faeries' only cattle. A faery lullaby called *Bainne nam fiadh* (deer's milk) suggests that milk from hinds substituted for faery mothers' weakness in breastfeeding:

---

43 Jamieson. *Northern Antiquities.* (1814) pp405–406.

"On milk of deer I was raised,
On milk of deer I was nurtured,
On milk of deer beneath the ridge of storms,
On crest of hill and mountain."[44]

These milk-herds may be found under the supervision not just of faery women (*bean sith*) – like the banshee of Glen Nevis who is often seen driving and milking her deer – but also *glaistigs* and various so-called 'hags'. Given how easily deer are startled and scared off by humans, it will be clear how close a connection these supernatural herders must have with the livestock, even though (to us) they may appear repulsive and scary. Faery women can often take on the form of deer as well.[45]

The huge hag called *cailleach-uisge,* the water woman, lives in remote, mountainous places, and acts as a guardian to many wild animals, especially deer, which she herds and milks on the mountains. Normally, it is considered bad luck for a hunter to see her but occasionally she may allow one of her deer to be hunted by favoured individuals; the same is true of other faery herders.[46]

The Highland hag called the *cailleach bheur* was mentioned earlier for her control over the weather, but she also keeps large flocks of deer, cattle and pigs and, on winter nights, at a time when other grazing is in short supply, she may sometimes be seen driving her deer down onto beaches of Mull where they can feed on the seaweed. By way of contrast, the Carlin Wife of the Spotted Hill (*Cailleach Beinne Bhric horo*) has a herd which, it is said,

44 Campbell. *Superstitions*. p28; Mackenzie. *Scottish Folklore*. pp204–205; Carmichael. *Carmina Gadelica*. Vol.2. p232.
45 Campbell. *Superstitions*, pp28, 50, 90, 109 & 126.
46 Campbell. *Superstitions*. p122.

she will *not* allow to descend to the beach; instead, they "love the water-cresses by the fountain high in the hills better than the black weeds of the shore." The 'Woman of Mist' of Bicknoller Hill in the western Quantock Hills of Somerset is a rare southern example of a faery woman who herds deer.[47]

OTHER FAERY ANIMALS

As I just noted, the *cailleachbheur* keeps pigs along with her other livestock and is generally regarded as a protector of swine. In her role as a controller of weather, the *cailleach* apparently rides astride storm-bringing hogs. The Gyre Carlin in Fife is said to be accompanied by her pig and can even take pig form if she wishes. Such a guise for a supernatural may also be encountered on the Isle of Man. In 1910, the Reverend Canon Kewley, of Arbory parish on the island, recounted the experience of a staunch Methodist he knew. This man had once seen the road full of little black pigs which all vanished as soon as he demanded of them, "In the name of God, what are ye?" He was quite sure that he had seen a group of the 'little folk'.[48]

To protect herds of cattle against faery threats in the Scottish Highlands, a prayer or spell would be recited by a farmer:

> "From every *gruagach* and banshee,
> From every evil wish and sorrow,
> From every *glaistig* and *bean nighe*,

---

47 Mackenzie. *Scottish Folklore*. p152; Campbell. *Superstitions*. p29; Also see my *Beyond Faery*. c.7.
48 Mackenzie. *Scottish Folklore*. pp148–152; Evans Wentz. *Fairy Faith*. p126.

From every fairy-mouse and grass mouse,
Oh, save me to the end of my day."

The two rodents mentioned are the *lucha-sith* and the *luch-feoir.* The first animal, the fairy mouse, is the lesser shrew, a mammal that was much disliked in the Highlands because it was thought to run across animals when they were lying down and blight their spines, or across humans when asleep, paralysing their arms. This a condition is known as *marcadh sith* or 'faery riding'; the phrase also denoted the sweating observed in weak and unhealthy stock

The latter 'mouse' is in fact the common shrew. If one is caught, it is rolled up in a cloth and kept to be used to treat paralysis in livestock. Ideally it should still be alive to work the best cures; it is carried clockwise around an affected beast, invoking the trinity. The same ritual was performed with the *lucha sith,* whether alive or dead. In addition, if seen near a house, the *luch-feoir* was dreaded as a sign of imminent death.[49]

FAIRIES AND INSECTS

Faeries are traditionally quite small (child sized, typically). In recent centuries, though, they have been miniaturised in popular culture and, in addition, they have acquired wings, making their potential similarities to insects inevitable. Many modern reports explicitly identify faeries with insects such as butterflies and dragonflies. However, the links go far deeper than a mere surface resemblance.

49 Carmichael. *Carmina Gadelica.* Vol.2. p323 & Vol.1. p31; Mackenzie. *Scottish Folklore.* p204.

Bees

There is some strange connection between the faes and bees which, rather like their associations with the cuckoo, are now no longer as clear to us as once may have been the case. As an illustration, in the 1641 poem, *The Parliament of Bees,* poet John Day makes Obron the King of the Bees and fairies act as his servants. Describing Welsh fairies, one twentieth century folklorist was very definite about their close connection with bees. He described the insects as being "the messengers of the fairies and [they] will lead you to them and their habitats ... where the bees toil, there are the fairies."[50]

There is certainly a perceived similarity in terms of appearance and sound between insect and supernatural. Manx folklorist Dora Broome twice described the little folk as looking "like a swarm of bees." In another example, a man on Arran was out cutting bracken one day when the fairy host flew over him. He reported that he saw "something like a swarm of bees," into which he threw his reaping hook. The iron tool caused the faes to drop his wife, whom they had abducted, after leaving a 'stock' behind in her bed. A man working his garden at Breadalbane was beset by a crowd of men and women "who appeared to him skimming over the tops of the unbending corn and mingling together like bees going to hive." Similarly, in the Cornish tale of the *'Miser on St Just Gump,'* he is set upon by the pixies for trespassing upon their revels:

> "Whirr! Whirr! Whirr! As if a flight of bees were passing him, buzzed in his ears ... he felt as if a

---

50 Ellis, T.P. 'Welsh Fairies' in *Welsh Outlook*. Vol.16, No.10 (1929) p297.

number of insects were running over him, and by the light of the moon he saw standing on his nose one of the spriggans, who looked exceedingly like a small dragon-fly."[51]

As well as the motion in flight, the noise of the fairies might resemble that of a hive of bees. John Aubrey told a tale of his former schoolmaster, Mr Hart, who in 1633 came across a "faiery dance" (a green circle on the grass) on the Wiltshire Downs and saw there sprites who were "making all manner of odd noyses." They objected to his intrusion on their dancing and swarmed at him, "making a quick humming noyse all the time." A fairy host described on the Isle of Man sounded first like humming bees, then like a waterfall, and lastly resembled a marching and murmuring crowd as they drew progressively nearer to the witness.[52]

Staying with the Manx faes, another traditional belief was that 'bumbees' are actually misbehaving fairies who have been turned into insects as a punishment by others in their community. In Ireland, in the 1850s, a folklore collector was told that bees are fairies, who are in turn the souls of those deceased, a notion that connects us back to the longstanding ties between fairyland and the land of the dead. The identity between fairies and bees is attested from Wales, too. In *British Goblins*, Wirt Sikes described how those trying to destroy ancient megalithic monuments would face supernatural opposition, amongst which might be "swarms of bees, which are supposed to be fairies in disguise."[53]

51 Broome, *Manx Fairy Tales* – 67 and *More Manx Fairy Tales*. p40; MacKenzie, W. *The Book of Arran*. p258; Scott, Walter. *Letters on Demonology*. Letter 5.
52 Morrison, Sophia. *Manx Fairy Tales*, 'Billy Beg, Tom Beg & the Fairies.'
53 *Notes & Queries*. Vol.10 (1854) p500; Sikes. *British Goblins*. p383.

Lastly, mention ought to be made of the spirit called Browney, a Cornish fairy whom you'll find listed by Katherine Briggs amongst others. Simon Young (of the Fairy Investigation Society) has written an article, *Against Taxonomy: The Fairy Families of Cornwall*, which argues quite convincingly that this sprite – who was allegedly summoned to settle a swarm – was simply the product of confusion and misremembered stories, and never existed at all.

Moths

Just as similarities have been seen between fairies and bees, their associations with moths have also been recognised – and are probably even stronger.

Fluttering Faes

A lot of the material linking fairies with moths is highly romantic and literary. As popular opinion began to conceive of tiny winged fairies from the eighteenth century onwards, the association between fays and pretty insects made more and more sense. We might, in fact, date this connection from as early as the fairy character Moth in *A Midsummer Night's Dream*, although Dr Beachcombing on the *Strange History* website has argued that this is really a misreading for 'mote'.

The pairing between moths and faes has subsequently manifested itself in several ways in literature. Fairies acquired moth and butterfly wings, as we may see in many Victorian and later pictures; another source for these insect wings may come from classical representations of winged nymph Psyche. Instead of riding horses, fairies started to be imagined by nineteenth century poets and painters riding moths and flies. Julius Cawein mentions in 'Dream Road' "the moths they say the fairies use as coursers;" Alice Cary in 'Fairy folk' described fairies travelling "in coaches/That are drawn by butterflies." As the poetic faes drew closer to nature, in the process discussed in chapter two, they started to care for insects and other wildlife. In Menella Bute Smedley's poem 'The Butterfly and the Fairies,' it's the fays that make the butterfly's gorgeous painted wings whilst in Peter John Allan's 'The Dead Butterfly' Faery seems to be the lepidoptera heaven, where the deceased insect goes to dance with the 'elfin band'.

These conceits were taken to an extreme in the anonymous poem 'The Fairies' Fancy Ball,' published in 1832, in which the vernacular names of every species of butterfly and moth are played upon in a dream of a dance put on by the fairy queen. This evolution of the 'artistic faery,' as we might call it, directly informs our thinking today. If, for example, we look at the encounters reported in the recent Fairy Census, small flying fays are very common indeed and insect wings are a feature of quite a number of reports (see below).

Over and above these literary conceits, there is some decent folklore evidence linking faeries and moths. Our starting point is a brief remark by Robert Hunt in his Popular Romances of the West of England:

"Mr Thoms has noticed that in Cornwall 'the moths which some regard as departed souls, others as fairies, are called Pisgies.' This is somewhat too generally expressed; the belief respecting the moth, so far as I know, is confined to one or two varieties only.

Mr Couch informs us that the local name, around Polperro, of the weasel is *Fairy*. So that we have evidence of some sort of metempsychosis amongst the elf family. Moths, ants, and weasels it would seem are the forms taken by those wandering spirits."[54]

The Mr Thoms mentioned by Hunt wrote about 'The folklore of Shakespeare' in *The Athenaeum*, in 1847.[55] In this article he says little more than Hunt repeats, except to record that seeing the moths as pixies was the belief in the Truro area of mid-Cornwall, adding that it was thought that when the moths were very numerous, there would be great mortality to follow. It's also fascinating to learn that in Yorkshire the night flying moth *Hepialishumali* was called 'the soul' and that, in the Lake District too, moths were traditionally regarded as a sign of death.

There seems to be a link with death then, which is probably quite unsurprising if you think of a ghostly white moth seen at night. Equally, as I've described elsewhere, there are strong associations between fairies and death and it's another Cornish belief that the souls of unbaptised infants may become piskies. Evans Wentz was also told in 1910 that the local tin miners believed white moths to be spirits.[56]

There are some other fragments of folk belief to add to these tantalising remnants. According to J. Henry Harris, Cornish mothers used also tell their children that the little brown pisgie moth would play tricks on them in their sleep.[57] In her story of 'The Little Cake Bird,' North

54 Hunt, R. *Popular Romances of the West of England*. (1865) p82.
55 *Athenaeum*. (1847) No.1041, 1055.
56 Wentz. *Fairy Faith*. p183.
57 *Cornish Saints and Sinners*. (1907) c.20.

Cornish author, Enys Tregarthen, stated that the belief around St Columb is that the fairies will pass over your nose and arrange your dreams whilst you sleep. We know that Queen Mab is the faery midwife of dreams, so all of this seems to be interrelated.[58]

At St Nun's Well near Looe, on the south coast of the Cornish peninsula, there is a tradition of leaving a bent pin as an offering. If you fail to do this, you will be followed home by a cloud of the pisgey moths. We will examine fairies and wells in detail in the final chapter, but this particular local tradition underscores both that connection and the need to show proper respect by making offerings to the fairies.

Lastly, in a story from the Blackdown Hills of Somerset, a woman is brushed across her brow by a large moth and thereby receives the 'pixy-sight' which enables her to see an old pixy man who has come to ask for her skill in nursing his sick wife. We know fairy powers can be transferred by touch, so this again tallies with other lore, although the medium of the moth is unusual.[59]

Some Modern Evidence

The recent *Fairy Census* confirms that there is still felt to be some common association between fairies and lepidoptera. Some beings seen in Ohio flying around flowers were described as being "small, pale, with long limbs and wings similar to moths." A man waiting for a train in Scotland saw a small ball of light hovering around one of the platform lights:

58 See my *Famous Faeries*. (2020)
59 Mathews. *Tales of the Blackdown Borderland*. p59.

"At first, I thought it was a moth being illuminated but then realised that it was too big to be a moth and also it was very, very bright. It hovered for a few moments then shot across the platform and it joined another ball of light opposite."

He assumed it had to be a fairy because this was the "first thought that came into my head after I realised it wasn't moths."[60]

Several other contemporary witnesses made comparisons to butterflies: consider for instance a Texan sighting of "a beautiful butterfly with a lovely body of a lady," a "bright, white light about five foot long with wings like a butterfly and a short dress" or a being "like a white butterfly." Other sightings were compared to dragonflies and, in all instances, the witnesses paired insect wings with a humanoid body.[61]

'WHAT'S BEEN DID & WHAT'S BEEN HID:' ANIMALS & SECOND SIGHT

Humans' ability consistently to see fairies is poor. The ability is innate in a very few but otherwise must be acquired, which may happen in various ways. As we just saw, contact with a faery moth will transfer the vision, as will touching an endowed human, so long as the contact is maintained. Objects may convey the ability, such as a holed stone found on a fairy knoll, as may accidents: a man who entered a fairy knoll at Killin in Perthshire was splashed in

---

60 *Census.* Numbers 169 & 350; see too Johnson. *Seeing Fairies.* p235.
61 *Census.* Numbers 375, 419 & 435 (butterflies) and 16, 69, 190, 320 & 400 (dragonflies).

the eye by some porridge whilst he was there and forever after could see the faes. Similar is the experience of a man walking across the hills of Mull, who paused to bathe his feet with St John's wort and found the herb allowed him to see a fairy woman watching him. Certain rituals can acquire second sight, too, such as washing your face with the first egg of a chicken.[62]

In contrast, puzzlingly, animals seem to be far better at seeing fairies than we are. We know this from the reactions of pets and livestock – but have to assume that wild creatures are equally as aware of the supernatural beings around them. Martin, touring the Hebridean islands in the eighteenth century, reported the local belief that children, horses and cows were all endowed with the second sight and could see fairies. The inclusion of children in this list suggests that faery vision may be innate in humans, but that it is 'bred' out of us by education and social pressures.[63]

Animals, of course, don't suffer from the demands placed upon human infants to 'grow out' of faery belief and, as a result, they will see beings to which we have become oblivious. In one story from Northumberland, for example, a man's hunting dog would 'point' the fairies which were invisible to its master (although he could hear their music coming from a nearby green hillock).[64]

Cattle are aware, and seem to have no aversion to the creatures. For instance, the well-known story of 'The Little People's Cow' from Cornwall encapsulates many of the key aspects of the situation. The dairy maid only sees the

---

62 Campbell. *Superstitions*. pp15 & 103; Haldane Burgess. 'Some Shetland Folklore.' *Scottish Review*. Vol.25. (1895) p102.
63 Martin. *Description of the Western Isles*. p306.
64 Oliver. *Rambles in Northumberland*. p106.

fairies when she accidentally includes a four-leaf clover in her weise, the cushion of grass on which she rested the milk pail on her head. Then she witnesses:

> "A great number of little beings – as many as could get under Rosy's udder at once – held butter-cups, and other handy flowers or leaves, twisted into drinking vessels, to catch the shower of milk that fell among them, and some sucked it from clover-blossoms. As one set walked off satisfied, others took their places. They moved about so quickly that the milkmaid's head got almost 'light' whilst she looked at them. 'You should have seen,' said the maid afterwards – how pleased Rosy looked, as she tried to lick those on her neck who scratched her behind her horns, or picked ticks from her ears; whilst others, on her back smoothed down every hair of her coat. They made much of the calf, too; and, when they had their fill of milk, one and all in turn brought their little arms full of herbs to Rosy and her calf – how they licked all up and looked for more!"[65]

The human can only see the fairies with magical aid; the cow does not require this (unless, we might speculate, she has the benefit of eating the clover) and, in addition, there is a mutually rewarding relationship between cow and fays. A rather similar tale comes from the other end of England, from Nether Witton in Northumbria. A girl returning from milking with her pail on her head saw the fairies gambolling in the pastures although none of her

---

65 Bottrell. *Traditions and Hearthside Stories of West Cornwall.* Vol. 2. (1873) p73.

companions could see them. It was later realised that see too had unwittingly included four-leaved clover in her weise. Lastly, an old woman from Sutherland described in the 1930s how, as a little girl, she had gone with her mother to tend their cattle in the field one summer's evening. There, she could see small green people dancing around the legs of the cows, something that was hidden from her mother. Evidently, again, the cows were unperturbed by the faeries gambolling amongst them; we may note too that the child still retained her second sight at this stage.[66]

Horses, in contrast to cows, seem to be alarmed by fairies. In Yorkshire there was a tradition that boggarts would disguise themselves as stones on moorland tracks, deliberately to trip up passers-by. Horses, in particular, are able to see them better than people could – and often when they rear up unexpectedly it's because they have 'taken the boggart' – they are the aware of the presence of one, even if it doesn't look like a boggart. Something similar is reported from the Isle of Man. Here, there was once no bread delivery at Orry's Dale because the baker's boy said that his cart horse was able to see the fairies after dark and would take fright. On this particular occasion, as it was getting near dusk, the boy had decided not to risk the horse rearing or bolting – and had gone home instead, leaving his customers hungry.[67]

These instances notwithstanding, there is also a little evidence for a relationship between horses and pixies akin to that just discussed with cows. Pixies and other little folk often take horses from stables and ride them at night

66 *Denham Tracts*.Vol.2. pp144–5; Oliver. *Rambles in Northumberland*. p106; Sutherland, G. *Folklore Gleanings*. (1937) p22.
67 Billingsley. *West Yorkshire Folk Tale*. p39; *Yn Lioar Manninagh*. Vol.III. p482.

until they are sweating and exhausted – a circumstance that doubtless heightens the steeds' wariness of their fae visitors, yet a few accounts suggest that they may enjoy this attention.[68]

SONGS FROM THE WOOD: THE FAERIES & TREES

"Trees that smell like a wind out of fairy-land,
Where little people live
Who need no geography
But trees."[69]

Many people see the faeries as a woodland folk, although (as we'll see later) across Britain, wooded areas are *not* the primary locations in which they live. This perception of the faes as a sylvan race is epitomised in the refrain of Sir Walter Scott's faery poem, *Alice Brand,* which celebrates how "Merry it is in the good greenwood,/When the mavis and merle are singing." Building upon classical concepts of dryads and other wood nymphs, Shakespeare's 'wood near Athens' in *A Midsummer Night's Dream* probably fixed this unjustified image in our minds. Nonetheless, the faeries certainly like glades for dancing – amongst other locations.

In the ballad *The Faerie Oak of Corriewater,* the elves appear as both users *and* propagators of woodland. The faery queen calls on her retinue to dance by the haunted oak, telling them that:

---

68 See my *British Pixies*. (2020) p78.
69 Conkling, Hilda. 'Geography,' in *Poems by a Little Girl*. (1920).

"I found the acorn on Heshbon Hill,
In the nook of a palmer's poke,
A thousand years since; here it grows!
And they danced till the greenwood shook..."

An important distinction must also be made between woods and timber – the product of felled trees. There are some woods that faery-kind can't abide: their aversion to rowan/mountain ash is very well-known. Atypical example comes from Durham, where it's said that a length of rowan wood bound with a red thread will scare off both bogles and witches. In fact, it is a more complex magical relationship than just a matter of avoidance. For example, a Scottish boy once made a whistle out of 'roddan' (rowan) wood and found that he could play "the scales of the in-between world music" on it. It had the power too of summoning to him a faery woman, who became his wife for seven years. The magic was time-limited, however, and at the end of this term she disappeared, despite his efforts to renew the enchantment by making a fresh whistle. It was a once in a lifetime spell, sadly.[70]

At the same time, though, faery links with certain groups of trees and with certain species of trees are very strong. Lewis Spence remarked that "Fairies, like the dead, frequently inhabit trees. If not actually worshipped, such trees are certainly regarded as sacred." He illustrated his statement by reference to Loch Shiant, the 'faery loch' on Skye, where there are the remains of a 'sacred grove', a place which was held in such reverence that no-one would take a twig from it.[71]

---

70 *www.tobarandualchais.co.uk* (March 1st 1980); Brockie, W. *Legends & Superstitions of the County of Durham.* (1886) p119.
71 Spence. *Fairy Tradition in Britain.* p321.

Trees are frequently the locations beneath which, or around which, the faeries dance. On the land of Sir Robert Vaughan at Dolgellau, for example, there stood a renowned oak, known locally as the 'Elf's Hollow Tree.' This close association can also manifest itself in the protection of trees from felling (as seen earlier), minor examples of which may be Tam Lin's ban upon the plucking of roses on the faery hill of Carterhaugh, Hynd Etin's similar disapproval of taking nuts and breaking branches in his role as 'guardian o' the wood,' and the prohibition against picking and removing flowers from a faery island in a lake near Brecon, which annually became visible on May Day – until the faes' hospitality was breached by one mortal visitor who took a posy home.[72]

In Scotland, the faeries are even more intimately associated with trees, figuring – as folklorist Donald MacKenzie said – as "tree spirits, not only as haunters of woodland but as actual tree dwellers." He substantiated this statement with two stories. Around 1812, a Highlander called Hugh Ross who lived near Lairg in Sutherland saw three women playing in a tree at the edge of one of his fields. Unwisely he decided to interfere and reproached them for their conduct, saying they ought to be at home doing their wifely chores. Although they were all dressed in green and behaving oddly, he did not realise they were faeries. One of the women climbed down and struck him in the face with a twig. He immediately fell to the ground but recovered enough to get home, where he took to his bed and soon afterwards died.[73]

72 Spence. *British Fairy Origins.* p186; Rhys. *Celtic Folklore.* p21; see too my *Faery* c.5.
73 MacKenzie. *Scottish Folklore.* p212.

It seems these women were some sort of 'dryad', they lived within the trees, rather than having just climbed up into the branches for fun. This intimate link to the life of a tree is brought far more clearly in Gaelic verse concerning a 'faery queen' who inhabited a tree.

"The maiden queen of wisdom dwelt,
In beauteous bower [literally, 'the bright sunshine'] of a single tree.
Where she could see the whole world,
And no fool could her beauty see."

Grieved at the lack of wisdom amongst mortal women, the faery queen summoned them to her by putting the 'fairy flax' to her lips, from which her message was transmitted through every plant, flower, bush and tree, calling all women to the faery knoll. The fairy flax, called *mungan* in Gaelic, is used medicinally to treat stomach ailments and is also called *lion na mnatha sithe*, 'the flax of the faery woman.' It acts as a safeguard against invisible dangers, as described in this invocation:

"Gorm-shùileach na mnà sìth
Gu mo dhion is gu mo chomhnadh
O'n a sluagh is o shith,
O mhighean is o dhòbheairt."

'The blue-eyed one of the fairy woman,
Serve to shield me and to keep me
From the hosts (of the air) and from faery,
From ill-will and from ill-deed.'

91

When the women of the world arrived in answer to her summons, the faery queen emerged from her tree, dressed in radiant green, and wisdom was dispensed to them from a limpet shell. Sadly, though, the numbers attending were so great that the cup ran dry and not all could be blessed in this way.[74]

Finally, 'wishing trees' are known across the Highlands. For example, on an island in Loch Maree that's known to be a place of faery assemblies, there grows a 'sacred' oak over a holy well which is visited by local people to make wishes; a nail is hammered into the tree to mark the act.[75]

We must also acknowledge that there can be a darker side to the faery relationship to vegetation. This was hinted at by the experience of Hugh Ross from Lairg. It is clearer if we consider the freshwater spirits such as Jenny Greenteeth and the Scottish Highland being called the *fideal*. These beings are intimately associated with the weeds and grasses that grow in and around bodies of water, with which the careless and unlucky can become entangled and drown. Nature, and the spirits that inhabit wild places, must be approached with respect and a healthy fear.[76]

Fairy Thorns

The faes are often associated with particular species of trees, notably hawthorns and – as we shall see – with elders. The importance of the hawthorn is confirmed by an early eighteenth century historian from Northumberland,

---

74 Carmichael. *Carmina Gadelica.* Vol.2. pp248–149 & Vol.3. p182.
75 MacKenzie. *Scottish Folklore.* p213.
76 See my *Beyond Faery.* (2020) c.2.

who reported that an old man had told him that "there was a time when there was not a solitary hawthorn tree, out on the green hills, standing amid its circuit of fine cropped grass, that was not witness to the fairy revel and dance held beneath its encircling branches in the twilight or by the pale light of the moon."

Respect for thorn trees and avoidance of damaging them is ingrained across the British Isles; for example, a Dumfriesshire ploughman who took great care to leave a large untilled circle around a thorn in the middle of a field was rewarded with a banquet, laid out at the end of his furrows. Central as thorns are to faery mythology, the stories directly concerning them are relatively few. The trees are often there, in the background, their presence signifying that there is something uncanny about the scene (just as is the case with meeting strangers dressed in green). An example from ballad is the thorn growing on the Eldritch Hill where *Sir Cawline* is required to fight the Eldritch knight. These trees are seldom the subject of an account, though – perhaps for the very reason that most individuals knew very well to steer clear of them.[77]

Fairies & Holly

Faeries and the magical qualities of holly feature in the North Welsh story of Merfyn Ffowc, a shepherd from Snowdonia. Merfyn got lost in a thick mist on the mountains near CwnLlan and, after wandering for some time, he heard a voice crying out in distress from higher

---

77 *Denham Tracts.* Vol.2. p136; Maxwell-Wood, J. *Witchcraft & Superstitious Record in the South Western District of Scotland.* (1911) p175; see my *Faery Ballads.* (2020).

above him. He clambered up a steep rock-face to find a small woman trapped in a cleft into which she had slipped. She was dressed in green, with silver shoes, and spoke a language he couldn't understand – evidently a fairy. He carried her down the cliff and, almost as soon as they had reached the bottom, two men appeared, calling out for 'Silifrit'. Appreciative of Merfyn's brave rescue, they presented him with a holly staff as a sign of their gratitude, and almost instantly vanished.

It turned out that this staff was lucky. Within the year, Merfyn married a rich widow and his flocks expanded amazingly: every ewe gave him two lambs. It seems, however, that he didn't fully appreciate (or recognise) the role of the fairy gift in his good fortune. As a result, he was caught one night in a terrible storm as he returned home from an evening drinking in Beddgelert and he lost his holly staff in the raging wind and rain. With the stick went all Merfyn's new prosperity: all his sheep were washed away in the same floods and he ended up poorer than he had started.[78]

The holly staff seems to have had a magical significance for the fairy donors – as other examples will show. The Welsh story immediately reminded me of another one, much older and from the other side of Britain. On June 17th 1499 in Norwich, John and Agnes Clerk and their daughter, Marion, appeared before a church court accused of sorcery. The family lived in Great Ashfield in Suffolk where the daughter had developed a reputation as a healer, soothsayer and finder of buried treasure. Marion immediately confessed everything, admitting that the

---

78 *Welsh Outlook – A Monthly Journal of National Social Progress.* Vol. 2. Issue 10 (October 1915), 'Snowdon Folklore.'

fairies helped her whenever she needed information. Amongst their assistance to her was the gift of a holly stick. Subsequently, her mother had taken it to the church on Palm Sunday, mixed up with the palm fronds, to be blessed, and Marion then used the stick to find treasure.

Two cases; two holly sticks from the faeries. What more do we know about the connection between this tree and the Good Folk? The plain answer has to be: not a lot. Katharine Briggs mentions in her *Dictionary of Fairies* that the holly is a fairy tree, along with the better known elder, oak and rowan, but she does not offer us more than this. In the traditional Scots ballad of *The Elfin Knight,* holly is mentioned in the refrain in two versions of the song: for example, "Sing green bush, holly and ivy." These two refrains strongly indicate a faery or supernatural association with the shrub without elucidating its nature.[79]

Robert Graves, in *The White Goddess,* gives a very full treatment of the magical and mythical significance of the shrub. He finds associations with the legends of King Arthur, Robin Hood and *Sir Gawain and the Green Knight.* He also traces much deeper Druidic, Classical and Biblical links. None of these are specifically fae, but the symbolic power of the tree seems very clear.

Reverting to British folklore, in the Scottish Highlands, holly is recorded as having been used to ward off the *sith* folk at New Year. Perhaps its potency derives from its prickles (cut gorse is used in another story to defend against the faeries), from its evergreen (and therefore 'immortal') qualities and from its red berries. Just as with the rowan, which is regularly used as a protection against faery attack, red is a very powerful and defensive colour.

---

79 See versions K & L in *Child's Ballads.*

A custom in Wales is for holly to be put out in inclement weather for the faeries to shelter in, but as we've just seen, in the Scottish Highlands, holly was used to decorate houses on New Year's Eve precisely because it kept the fairies out.[80]

On Jersey, the belief is that the local *faitiaux* venerate the holly tree and that, as a consequence, it should not be used to clean sooty chimneys. Conversely, again, in the Glencoe area it was thought that rowan and holly would both keep the fairies out of houses.[81]

Fairies & Elder

Elder trees are widely seen as having some sort of magical or spiritual properties. For example, in Herefordshire there was a taboo upon burning elder wood for fear of bringing misfortune, whilst its inner rind was used to cure cows of jaundice. Witches were said to dislike the tree, so its pith was fed to those believed to have been bewitched. In Shropshire elder was never used as firewood as it would bring misfortune, even death, to the household. The wood shouldn't even be brought into the house, as it could cause a cow to lose its calf, nor should cattle be driven with an elder stick. The juice of the plant would be used to protect the threshold and the hearth.

At the Rollright stone circle in Oxfordshire, an elder tree cut on Midsummer Eve would bleed and one of the stones would move its head. In Lincolnshire, it was said that a baby left in an elderwood crib would be pinched

---

80 *Carmarthen Weekly Reporter*. (April 19th 1918) p4, 'The Passing Week'; Campbell. *Superstitions*. p20.

81 John L'Amy. *Jersey Folklore*. (1927) p24; Fairweather, B. *Folklore of Glencoe*. (1974) p1.

black and blue (doubtless by avenging faes) and people would avoid cutting wood from live trees, although dead, dry wood was safe to work with or burn.[82] In the nearby Cotswolds, elders were alleged to be witches' trees, their bleeding when cut being the result of the fact that they were women disguised in tree form. This explains why furniture, especially cribs, ought not to be made from the tree. Another local tradition was that fairies hid under elders from witches.[83]

In county Durham, a branch of the 'bur tree' (elder) guards against both witches and fairies. Its juice gives the second sight. An elder stick in the pocket will protect a horse and rider from harm on a long journey and, if you strike a horse with an elder stick and then bind the wand to its belly, it will not 'stale'. Renowned widely as a tree that repels flies, beating another tree with a piece of elder will make the other fly free as well.[84]

On the Isle of Man, the same ideas prevailed as on the British mainland. Whilst the tree was said to be the haunt of the fairies, it repelled witches and, accordingly, there was hardly to be found an old well (*tholtan* in Manx) near which there didn't grow an elder tree, according to Agnes Herbert in a guide to the island written in 1909. If you carried elder leaves with you, the islanders believed, you would be protected against witchcraft.

These are but the first indications of the supernatural associations of the *tramman* tree on the island. The fairies live in the trees (especially when they are far from the hills) and when the branches of the trees are seen to bend

82 Hull, E. *Folklore of the British Isles.* pp131 & 133.
83 Briggs, K. *Folklore of the Cotswolds.* (1974) p121.
84 Brockie, W. *Legends & Superstitions of the County of Durham.* (1886) p114.

in the wind at night, it is in fact the fairies riding upon them. Given their status as fairy residences, interference with the trees can be dangerous. Evans Wentz heard the story of a woman from Arbory parish who one dark night accidentally collided with a *tramman*. She was instantly smitten with a terrible swelling which all her neighbours agreed was the consequence of offending the fays by her clumsiness. Another local account told of a man who cut down an elder and was driven to suicide by the aggrieved fairies, Walter Gill recorded in 1932.[85]

The little folks' connection to the trees is emotional as well as purely functional. Thus, when the elders at Ballaboy were felled, the fairies came at night to lament their loss. A large crowd assembled and, in their heightened state, violent fighting broke out amongst them. Similarly, if the trees become decayed and the best branches for swinging on fall off, the fairies will abandon a location.[86]

The Manx fairies living in the 'tramman' are plainly very similar to the spirit called the Old Lady of the Elder tree who's known in the east of England and who must be appeased before wood is taken from the shrub. A kind of postponed sacrifice is promised, with the Old Lady's permission sought on the basis that, when the person is dead and buried, she can take wood growing on the speaker's grave. It's not clear, though, whether or not the faeries and the tree are identical. The Old Lady seems to personify the tree in some way – to be its soul – whilst the Manx fays live in, or at least gather in, the elders, but may not actually embody them. Regardless of the detail,

---

85 *Mannin*. No.3. (1913) p2.
86 *Proceedings of the Isle of Man Natural History & Archaeological Society*. Vol.1. (Jan,1889); *Manx Notes & Queries*. (1904) p125.

the supernatural associations are very clear and persistent and – what's more – can be seen across Northern Europe from Denmark to the British Isles.[87]

'From the Witchwood' – Faeries as Tree Spirits

Some of the manifestations of faes associated with trees suggest that they are, to some degree or other, the spirits that actually inhabit those plants – the British equivalents of the classical dryads, perhaps.

This is the case with the Old Lady of the Elder and, very possibly, with the fairy queen who lived in a Scottish tree standing on a knoll and dispensed wisdom the women of the world. In another Scottish example, an elderly woman interviewed in late Victorian times on Barra claimed often to have seen 'tree spirits,' dressed in (or coloured) green and playing amongst the trees.[88]

English orchards and nut groves are haunted by sprites whose role is to bring life to the trees and to protect the fruit from thefts.[89] This benign influence over the productivity and security of fruit and nut trees might be considered in the wider faery role of promoting fertility that I discussed in chapter two. However, these spirits appear to be inseparable from their trees so that thinking of them as indwelling may be a more accurate way of conceiving of them. These faeries go by various regional names, including Jack up the Orchard, the grig and the apple tree man. Ceremonies used to be conducted in

---

87 Briggs. *Dictionary of Fairies*. 'Old Lady'; see too my *Faery*. (2020) c.5.
88 Spence. *British Fairy Origins*. p100; Carmichael. *Carmina Gadelica*. Vol.2. p248.
89 Compare the Greek *nymphae epimelides*, the nymphs of meadows, pastures and orchards.

winter to 'wassail the trees' with libations of cider so as to encourage their growth. At harvest time in Somerset a few apples would always be left behind on the trees, which would be regarded as pixie-property. This customary offering was called 'pixying', 'grigging' or the 'pixy-hoarding' and in return it was hoped that the next year's crop would be blessed. The traditional Yuletide rituals address the 'old apple tree,' but surely this must denote not the mere organism but a life or spirit within it. The autumn gifts of apples far more explicitly acknowledge the vital faery presence in the trees.[90]

Fruit tree spirits are found across England. One writer listed the following:

"Churn-milk Peg (West Yorkshire & Malham, North Yorkshire) and Melsh Dick (north country) are wood-demons supposed to protect soft, unripe nuts from being gathered by naughty children, the former being wont to beguile her leisure by smoking a pipe. The Gooseberry-wife (Isle of Wight), in the guise of a large furry caterpillar, takes charge of the green gooseberries, hence 'If ye goos out in the gearden, the gooseberry-wife'll be sure to ketch ye'; while in the orchards is Awd Goggie (East Yorkshire), guarding the unripe apples."

Another writer describes Awd Goggie as a wicked sprite and adds that children are warned to stay away from orchards at "improper times" otherwise (just like the gooseberry wife) "Awd Goggie might get them." We can

---

90 See Sykes, Homer, *Once a Year.* (1977); Tongue, R. *Somerset Folklore.* (1965) p119; see also my *Faery.* (2020) c.5.

also add to this list Nut Nan, who guards the hazels from theft with threats of burning naughty children with heated pokers. Peg is described as being an old and very ugly hag, whose name derives from the hazels in their green state, when they're called 'churn-milk'. All she says is "Smoke! smoke a wooden pipe!/Getting nuts before they're ripe!" And if this doesn't work, she'll abduct the disobedient youths. Melsh Dick apparently derives his name from the same unripe, 'mushy' or 'mulchy' nuts; he too will make off with disobedient children. All of these northern sprites were assisted by Clap-Cans, a being with no form or substance whose sole purpose is to scare away youngsters by beating on tins with sticks.[91]

In the south of England, Lazy Lawrence haunted orchards from Hampshire to Somerset. In the former it seems that, rather like the colt-pixy or cole-pexyin of Dorset, he might take the form of a horse and chase naughty children and apple thieves.[92] In Somerset, Lawrence inflicted crippling ailments on anyone detected stealing the fruit. One spell used by farmers to protect their crops wished on the intruders that:

> "Starke be their sinews…
> May dread and doubt
> Enclose them about…
> So be the cramp in the toes
> Cramp and crooking
> And fault in their footing."[93]

---

91 Wright. *Rustic Speech & Folklore.* (1913) p198; Gutch. *County Folklore (East Yorkshire)*, Vol. 6. p40.

92 Brand. *Popular Antiquities.* Vol.2. pp512–513.

93 British Library Add MS 36674 or Halliwell, J.O. *Popular Rhymes & Nursery Tales.* pp273–274.

The thieves would become immobile and trapped, hence the rhyme "Lazy Laurence, let me goo/Don't hold me summer and winter too." Another Somerset proverb, "So many cratches [baskets], so many cradles," explicitly links fertility in the orchards and groves to fertility and growth in the human population.

These orchard spirits are sometimes termed 'nursery sprites' because of their particular role in stopping children 'scrumping' fruit and nuts before they are ready to be picked. This function was doubtless an important one, as it both protected the crops and avoided infants getting poorly eating unripe produce. Nevertheless, bearing in mind the fact that these beings are found only near their trees, the southern English customs of wassailing the trees, and the example of the Elder Woman, we may be justified in suspecting that the faeries of the orchards and groves had a more profound role in promoting growth and fruitfulness.[94]

FAERY & FUNGI

Mushrooms and toadstools are an essential element in faery rings (as I shall discuss in the next chapter), but the fae link to fungi is broader than this. For example, there is the substance widely known as fairy butter. At Upton, in West Yorkshire, it often used to be found in the mornings on rotten sticks and was thought to be a sign of good luck as well as being very good on boots and shoes. According to one report from the north-east of England, the butter was good to eat. A group of women, heading out early

---

94 Hole, C. *A Dictionary of British Folk Customs.* pp317–319.

into the fields for harvest, came across about one pound of butter on top of a gate post. They placed it in a basin and tried it later, declaring it to be "the nicest butter that any of them had ever tasted." Also from the same region come reports that children take by their parents into the fields at harvest times were warned away from the gathered stooks by telling them that the fairies would hide "baits" of butter amongst the sheaves, with the intention of kidnapping the youngsters. Implicit in this, of course, is the acceptance that the butter would be a tempting thing to eat.[95] In Wales a fungus called *y menyn y tylwyth teg* (fairy butter) used to be found by miners. It was said to be greasy (hence an alternative name of 'rock oil') and had an agreeable smell. It was found to help with rheumatism – being applied externally rather than being eaten, of course.[96]

Rather more romantically, it is said in Wales that mushrooms serve as fairy parasols.[97] Comparably, on the Isle of Man, a fungus that grows on elder trees is called 'fairies ears' or 'lugs', a substance it was unlucky to touch.[98]

95 *Leeds Mercury* (May 13th 1882) p1: 'Hazlethorpe Papers – Folklore;' *Denham Tracts*. Vol.2. p138.
96 *Bye Gones*, May (1878) p54 & October, p110.
97 Gwyndaf in Narvaez, 180.
98 *Mannin*. No.3. (1913) p2; Morrison, S. 'Manx Dialect Connected with Fairies.' *Proceedings of the Isle of Man Natural History and Archaeological Society*. Vol.1. New series (1906).

CHAPTER FOUR

Fairy Places in the Natural World

The faery world is not a wholly separate and unreachable place. It lies within and beneath the human world; it is integrated into our landscape, so that individuals from both sides of the border can pass over – voluntarily or not.

The fairies prefer a natural, undisturbed and unpolluted environment, hence the many reports of them fleeing all signs of human industrial progress, whether that is factories, trains or power and telephone lines. On Shetland, for example, the trows of the Knowe of Catfirth moved away when quarrying encroached on their homes.[1]

Perhaps it was a similar motivation that underlay the response of some of the *tylwyth teg* at Llanidloes, who found a man called Jack O'Leek pilfering firewood from trees and gave him the choice of how high he would like to be transported through the air over the land. In similar fashion, if a person damages the grass that grows beside Llyn Irddyn, they risk being abducted by the *tylwyth teg*.[2]

---

1 *Shetland News* (1903).
2 Harmer, E. 'Parochial Account of Llanidloes,' *Collections Historical & Archaeological Concerning Montgomeryshire*. Vol.10. (1877) p247; Rhys. *Celtic Folklore*. Vol.2. p148.

NATURAL HABITATS

"Ye elves of hills, brooks, standing lakes and groves,
And ye, that on the sand, with printless foot do
chase..."[3]

The faeries are almost exclusively an outdoor, rural people and, within the overall landscape of Britain, there are certain places specially designated or set apart for them. These reserved sites might be intended for the living or for their dead.[4]

The range of locations the faeries inhabit are illustrated very well by reviewing the evidence provided by Welsh informants to Professor John Rhys when he was compiling his *Celtic Folklore*, published in 1901. A variety of locations were identified, but there is a consistency of theme and preference underlying all of them.

The *tylwyth teg* live beneath a bottomless pool at Corwrion, Upper Arllechwedd – although they have fields and pastures surrounding the pool, which they have been seen farming. They are also known to live beneath Llyn Cynnwch.[5]

Caves are another preferred location, as in the Foel between Cwm Strallynand the upper Pennant Valley in Gwynedd and around Merthyr Tydfil in Glamorgan. Wholly subterranean dwellings are also known, for which entrances exist in the Fairy Glen near Bettws and under many river banks. Rhys records this description of the *tylwyth teg's* habitations from one of his many witnesses, William Jones of Beddgelert:

---

3   Shakespeare, W. *The Tempest*. Act 5, scene 1.
4   Spence. *British Fairy Origins*. p187.
5   Rhys. *Celtic Folklore*. pp52–53 & 136.

"It appears that the places most frequently resorted to by this species were rushy combes surrounded by smooth hills with round tops, also the banks of rivers and the borders of lakes; but they were seldom seen at any time near rocks or cliffs. So, more tales about them are found in districts of the former description than anywhere else, and among them may be mentioned Penmachno, Dolwyddelan, the sides of Moel Siabod,Llandegai Mountain, and from there to Llanberis, to Nantlle Lakes, to MoelTryfan and Nant y Bettws, the upper portion of the parish of Beddgelert from Drws y Coed to the Pennant, and the district beginning from there and including the level part of Eifion, on towards CelynnogFawr. I have very little doubt that there are many traditions about them in the neighbourhood of the Eifl and inLleyn; I know but little, however, about these last. This kind of fairies was said to live underground, and the way to their country lay under hollow banks that overhung the deepest parts of the lakes, or the deepest pools in the rivers, so that mortals could not follow them further than the water, should they try to go after them."[6]

What characterises all these locations is their inaccessibility to humankind. The same security from spying and interference could be achieved almost as well through remoteness. Hence, Rhys also recorded that the *tylwyth* much frequented the mountains of Dyfed, where they would shelter under ferns in summer and beneath heather and gorse in the winter (I'll discuss the preference for Welsh hills again later). They were known too to live on

---

6 Rhys. pp84–85, 96, 176, 205, 227 & 258.

an invisible island, described by the few who had got there as a 'paradise' in a lake in the Brecon Beacons. Their off-shore islands along the Welsh coast, the 'Green Spots of the Floods,' were also known to coastal dwellers and seafarers but they were largely invisible and inaccessible, except to the very lucky or favoured few.[7]

By way of contrast, the *tylwyth's* dancing and assemblies almost always took place on the earth surface. For purely practical reasons of convenience, open, level areas were selected, preferred locations being meadows, pastures, oat fields (presumably after reaping) and woodland glades.[8]

The situation does not appear to be very different in the Highlands of Scotland. J.G. Campbell summarised the evidence as follows. On the whole, the *sith* folk live in small hillocks generally called *sithein* or *tolman*. Such a hill may be distinguished "from the surrounding scenery by the peculiarly green appearance and rounded form. Sometimes in these respects it is very striking, being of so nearly conical a form, and covered with such rich verdure, that a second look is required to satisfy the observer it is not artificial." He added that:

> "Even lofty hills have been represented as tenanted by fairies, and the highest point of a hill, having the rounded form characteristic of fairy dwellings, is called its shi-en (*sithein na beinne*). Rocks may be tenanted by the elves, but not caves. The dwellings of the race are below the outside or *superficies* of the earth and tales representing the contrary may be looked upon with suspicion as modern. There is

7 Rhys. pp152, 20, 82 & 169–173; see also my *Faery* (2020). c.5.
8 Rhys. 50, 71 & 83.

[nevertheless] one genuine story in which the fairy dwelling is in the middle of a green plain, without any elevation to mark its site beyond a horse-skull, the eye-sockets of which were used as the fairy chimney."[9]

Just as in Wales, concealment appears to be a major element in the *sith's* preference for the knowes or knolls. As Campbell observed, a "fairy hillock might be passed by strangers without suspicion of its being tenanted." Of course, this protects the inhabitants' privacy but from time to time it can also lead to unwitting trespasses by humans, who pasture cattle or strip turf from the hill without realising that they are antagonising its invisible occupants – who are a people whom you would wish not to upset intentionally.

It's generally very well known that fairies live under hills, particularly in the north of England and in Scotland and, in fact, humans will sometimes enter those hills as well. People may be asked in – or wander in – to join dances; midwives and wet nurses are regularly invited in to help with births and child care, and some folk will have the misfortune to be abducted inside the hills. As just described, by their unique shape, lushness and isolation, the knolls stand out as separate and unusual features in the landscape and this ought really to act as a warning to people to keep well away. It doesn't always work this way, though, and, although there are stories of humans rewarded for showing respect to faery hillocks, there are more concerning people who've violated them.

As illustration, in the Highlands an old man kept the hillock near his house very clean by clearing from it any

9 Campbell. *Superstitions.* p12.

animal droppings or other dirt. He did this mainly because he liked to sit on the hill on summer evenings, but one dusk a small man whom he did not know appeared and thanked him for his care. In return, the stranger promised that if the man's cattle should stray at night, they would be kept out of the crops. A second farmer, who always avoided pasturing his horses and cows on a hillock and resisted taking turf from the knoll, was rewarded by the faes who would drive his livestock to shelter whenever a storm arose at night. By way of contrast, a man on Coll went to pull brambles from a faery knowe but heard someone call out angrily to him from inside. He ran away in fright.[10]

GREEN FAERY PLACES

As well as fairy habitations, there are also certain locations within the landscape that are reserved for the fairy dead. For example, it used to be widely believed in the north of England that any green shady spot was a fairy burial ground. Such locations obviously need to be shown the proper regard. In 1847, it was reported in the Manx newspaper *Mona's Herald* that a man called Quayle, living at Maughold on the island, had had his house windows broken by the faes because he had ploughed up some land never before cultivated and, in so doing, had turned up bones from an old grave yard. In just the same way, at Burrafield on Unst, there was a piece of land called the 'Field of the Dead.' Traditionally, it could not be cultivated without incurring misfortune. A woman decided to brave

---

10 Campbell. *Superstitions*. pp93, 95 & 96.

the warnings and dug up part of the field. Her cow died, but she was still not discouraged and sowed a crop of corn the following year. Her husband then died, after which she finally got the message.[11]

It's not just a matter of respecting sites already selected by the faes, though. Some may be deliberately granted to them by human communities. In Gloucestershire, presumably valuable agricultural land was given up to the fairies' sole occupation and use: when the fields at Upton St Leonard's were enclosed, an area called No Nation was set aside for the faeries' exclusive use and tall trees were left in the new hedgerows as places in which the fays could hide. This is a good example of humans showing the proper respect for the Good Folk, both appeasing them and adapting to living alongside them.[12]

As I described in chapter two, there was a much broader and deeper tradition of Scotland of allocating land to the faeries, a practice that the kirk struggled to suppress. In Berwickshire, on the Scottish border with England, areas called Clootie's Craft (or croft) and Goodman's Field were set aside by villagers and were never tilled or cropped by the human population. Even into the nineteenth century, these practices continued. Sir James Simpson, who pioneered the use of chloroform, recorded how in 1861 his great uncle had bought a farm at Gormyre in West Lothian and:

> "Among his first acts after taking possession was the enclosing of a small triangular corner of one of the fields within a stone wall. The corner cut off – which

11 Moore. *Folklore.* c.3; Edmondston. *Home of a Naturalist.* p224.
12 Palmer. *Gloucestershire.* p145.

remains to this day in the same state – was the 'Goodman's Croft.'"

Admittedly, it may have been the roughest and stoniest land on the farm, but the effort of making the wall alone indicates Simpson's cautious respect.[13]

It was considered extremely unlucky to dig or plough on these reserved portions (just as fairy rings should never be disturbed), for:

"He who tills the fairies' green
Nae luck again shall hae."

There was a further saying that, "If you put a spade in the Goodman's craft ... [the Devil] will shoot you with his shaft." Another rhyme, composed to warn locals against reckless cultivation, advised that:

"The craft lies bonny by Langton Lees
And is well liked by birds and bees.
If you plough it up, it'll be your death,
For disturbing the sod where the fairies like to tread."[14]

We even have a record of a local cunning man apparently involved in allocating an area of ground for this purpose. Andro Man, who was tried for witchcraft in Aberdeen in 1597, was reported to have "mett and messuritdyvers pieces of land, callitwardis, to the hyndknichtquhom thou confessis to be a spreit." In Scots, the term 'hyndknicht' might mean something like 'gentle knight' and may

---

13 Simpson, E.B. *Sir James Young Simpson.* (1896) pp21–22.
14 Henderson, G. *Popular Rhymes... of the County of Berwick.* p111.

therefore indicate Man's respect for the spirit in question (a usage comparable to 'Good Folk' or 'Good Neighbours'). Whatever the exact meaning of the term 'hyndknicht', this farming land was plainly being set aside for some supernatural being, whether we choose to label that entity a faery or a demon.

Throughout Britain, then, there has been a habit of preserving some land for the supernatural. This may have been the poorest plot on a farm, but the donation of an area of land seems to have been more important than its actual fertility. This may have been expressed differently from place to place: for example, in West Lothian a small field called 'Heelie Man's Rig,' 'the Old Man's Fold' or the 'Guide Man's Croft' or 'Acre' was walled about and left uncultivated, it was said for the devil. However it was that the plot was labelled, it was understood that communities must share and accommodate with the denizens of the otherworld. The only way in which this protection or proprietorship might be violated was a very human and commercial one: a payment of a sum of money to the fairies would be accepted as adequate compensation.[15]

FAIRY PORTALS

As we have seen, faeryland is generally located underground, from which it follows that there are entrances – portals where a human might gain access or is most likely encounter a fay being. In fact, there are both liminal locations and times of the day when it becomes much easier to see fairies or to enter fairyland.

15 Hendrie, W. *West Lothian Lore*. p15; *Old Statistical Account of Scotland*. Vol.21. (1799) Appendix for Monquhitter, Aberdeen. p148.

Portal Places

The folklore, literary sources and popular ballads are very consistent in the identifying the sorts of places or environments in which a meeting with a fae is likely. What appears to unify the locations is the fact that they all share a solitary or unique feature: they will stand out in the landscape.

A number of distinctive sites may be watched out for. Any lone tree standing isolated in a prominent position is noticeable and memorable in any case, but very often they mark a fae portal. For instance, Thomas of Erceldoune met the fairy queen at the 'Eildon tree' (in one version of the poem it is described as a "dern tree" – that is 'hidden' or 'secret'). In the romance of the same name, knight Sir Launfal is approached by two fairy maidens whilst sitting in the shade of a tree one hot *undrentide* during the feast of Trinity (late May or early June). In the Scottish ballad of *Allison Gross,* a man is turned into a dragon (or 'worm') by witch Alison and is left to coil himself around a tree. Lone trees are magical, definitely. However, we can go further and suggest that these fairy trees are very likely to be either may (or hawthorn) trees, which we know are notorious fairy haunts, and apple trees. In the ballad of *Young Tamlane* he's carried off by the elfin queen having fallen asleep underneath an apple and the wife of *Sir Orfeo* is stolen away from her husband by the fairies whilst sitting one early May morning in an orchard, beneath an "ympe tree" – a grafted apple.

As we shall see later, fairies are well known to live under burial mounds and isolated hillocks, but it appears that distinct and conspicuous hills of any description will be likely fairy spots at which contact can be made.

English poets Thomas Campion and Thomas Browne both imagined the fairy queen regally seated upon a grassy knoll (in the latter case surrounded too by a faery ring), whilst in folklore many everyday activities conducted upon a fairy hill could prove dangerous for humans, whether that was cutting turf, sitting, playing or just sleeping.[16]

Grassy banks and slopes are often mentioned specifically, but these features could very well just be part of a fairy hill rather than a separate element in the landscape – it's not always clear. Thomas of Erceldoune lay down on Huntlie bank on a May morning; in the ballad of *Thomas the Rhymer* we hear that he reclines on a grassy bank. There's a definite suggestion that part of the process may involve a tired person lying down to rest in the heat, drifting off to sleep, and, in that semi-conscious state, being able to make contact with faery. In the medieval poem *Piers Plowman* the narrator is out on the Malvern Hills on a May morning; "weori of wandringe" he went to rest "undur a brodbanke bi a bournesyde." It is then that he beholds "a ferly – a feyrie" (a wonder of fairy origin). In Edmund Spencer's poem, *The Faery Queen*, Prince Arthur similarly lies down to sleep on verdant grass after wandering in a forest and has a vision of the Fairy Queen lying down beside him. Elsewhere in his epic, Spenser imagines that "Nymphes and Faeries by banckes did sit;" there is clearly a close association here between faes and these slightly secluded locations.[17]

Finally, the magical communion with Faery is further enhanced, it seems, it there are daisies on the bank. In

---

16 Campion. *All Ladies That do Sleep*; Browne. *Britannia's Pastorals*. Book I, Song II, Lines 396–404.

17 Spenser. Book I, canto IX, stanzas 13–14 & Book I, canto X, stanza 65.

Allison Gross the fairy queen comes to sit on a "gowany bank" near to where the frightful worm coils about the tree. It may be significant too that in the ballad of *Lady Isabel and the Elf Knight* the wicked knight comes to the maid when she sits in her bower on the first of May, surrounded by daisies. They are one of the archetypal fairy flowers.

It will be evident from these examples that, whilst the place is important, the time of day (*undrentide*) and the time of year (very typically early May/Beltane) are also highly significant in bringing about an encounter. Contact seems to be more likely to occur at the hottest times of day and in the hotter seasons of the year. Combine all the right factors and a meeting with a faery is a very strong possibility.

Hours and Days

> "It was between the night and day
> When the Fairy King has power
> That I sunk down in a sinful fray
> And 'twixt life and death was snatched away
> To the joyless Elfin bower."[18]

Transitional times between morning and afternoon and between day and night are especially magical and perilous. For example, in *Beware the Cat,* written in 1584, William Baldwin mentioned "the Goblins houre," explaining that, "After one o'clock at midnight the goblines go abroad and as soon as any cock croweth, which is the houre at three, they retire homeward." I want here to focus here on one particular liminal hour – that of midday.

18 Scott, Walter. *The Lady of the Lake*, canto IV.

In the medieval poem *Sir Orfeo* the knight's lady, Dame Heurodyce, falls into the power of the king of fairy by unwisely sleeping at midday. She "went in an undrentide/ To play bi an orchardside" with her waiting women and then fell asleep until "that undrentide was al ydoune." *Underntide* is the late noon and early afternoon – perhaps the hottest and sleepiest time of day. Whilst Heurodyce slept, she was transported to Faerie and upon waking was dismayed to find herself back in the mortal world yet facing permanent abduction the following day.

A few of the Scottish witch trials also demonstrate the significance of 'boundary times' of day when you are passing from one part of the day to another or from day to night. Accused witch Catharine Caray met a 'great number of fairy men' near some fairy hills at sunset and Elspeth Reoch met a fairy man whom she had previously known in life – and who had been murdered at sunset. Dorset witchcraft suspect John Walsh visited the fairy hills near his home either at midday or midnight in order to get advice and instruction from the fairies.[19]

It's well known to be hazardous to sleep on fairy hills; this is doubly the case if you choose to slumber in the middle of the day. Here's a salutary tale from Shetland:

> "a young woman was dangerously ill. She had a fever, caught by falling asleep at midday on top of a little hill. She died and her father insisted that the fairies had possessed her and left a stock in her place. He could not be convinced otherwise and smiled at the foolishness of those who denied the fairies."[20]

19 Dalyell. *Darker Superstitions*. p536; Black. *Examples of Printed Folklore... Orkney*. p111.
20 Edmondston, Arthur. *A View ... of the Zetland Islands*, 1809, vol.2, 77.

It's fair to add that another Scottish source records how a child who slept on a *sithbruaich* (fairy hill) was not taken but was instead endowed with the second sight.[21]

There are, therefore, various landscape features, times, days and activities at which the human and the fairy world intersect. Most of these are chosen and initiated by the faes themselves: their intrusion into the mortal world to dance in rings, to abduct children (or adults) and to play music are good examples of these. Sometimes, though, we can discover what are often now termed 'portal' places and, for that matter, times, when the boundaries are weaker or thinner than is usually the case. With the right intersection of geographical and meteorological conditions, access to Faery can become easier, although it may continue to be a matter of chance and still be dependent on the faeries' choice.

SPECIAL FAIRY SITES

Fairies are often associated with particular locations in the landscape, such as ancient monuments, but how exactly are they linked to these sites?

'Living in the Past' – Barrows and Standing Stones

"I am struck by the fact that the fairies are not infrequently located on or near ancient sites..." said Professor John Rhys. There is, indeed, a very strong and longstanding link between faeries, megalithic structures and ancient burial tumuli. It may seem strange to discuss man-made

21 MacDougall & Calder. *Folk Tales and Fairy Lore in Gaelic.* (1910) p183.

structures, however old, as part of a discussion of the natural world, but I think it can be justifiable. Ancient structures connect us to 'the ancients' and enhance the sense that the faeries are timeless and permanent in the landscape. The fact that the ruins they now inhabit are long disused and have been abandoned to nature is part of their mystery – and hence that of their current inhabitants – and at the same time the re-absorption of the sites into the landscape tends to eradicate their 'artificial' character and operates to equate them with geological features such as hillocks and rock outcrops.[22]

The exact nature and purpose of the faery occupation of these sites, nevertheless, is a little uncertain. It's not always clear if the faes are merely present at the ancient monuments from time to time (usually to dance) or whether they actually reside at – or under – them. In some cases, the locations appear to be places where the faeries work their magic or where, at least, those magic powers linger.

For example, at the Rollright Stones in Oxfordshire, faeries who look like little girls have been seen dancing – but also disappearing down a hole by the King Stone, implying that they were accessing their underground home by that route. The Hurle Stane, near Chillingham in Northumberland, was another well-known site of faery assemblies, as was the 'Blue Stone' outside St Andrews in Fife and another large, flat stone in Berwickshire marked with the impression of a fairy foot. A well-known Welsh story concerns a shepherd boy of Frennifawr who saw a host of faeries dancing at an old cromlech. He was then

---

22 Rhys. *Celtic Folklore*. Vol.2. p674.

abducted by them, indicating how much fae activities are intertwined with ancient sites.[23]

On the Isle of Arran faeries meet at the various stone circles on the island, but they are especially closely linked to the megalithic complex at Machrie Moor: one of the stone circles there is a double ring called *Fion-gal's Cauldron Seat*. A faery or brownie was said to live below it – who was propitiated by pouring milk into a hole in the side of one of the stones. On North Ronaldsay, Orkney, it's reported that the trows celebrate the New Year by dancing in a circle around a menhir nine or ten feet tall and four feet broad which is also perforated (perhaps a single standing stone or all that remains of the portal to a burial chamber).[24]

It isn't just single or grouped standing stones, though. Prehistoric barrows also have very strong faery associations. The round barrow at Carn Gluze, St Just, Cornwall, is the place of faery dances and burning lights at night. The *fogou* called the Pisky House, which stands at Bosahan on the Helford River, was known for the unearthly noises that came from it; there is also a 'Pisky Hall' not far away at Trewardreva near Constantine. A long barrow at Butcombe in Somerset is called the Fairy Toot; another barrow in the same county at Stoke Courcy is known as the Pixies' Mound and yet another on Beaulieu Heath in Hampshire is called the Pixies' Cave. All these names strongly imply that our Good Neighbours were known to live beneath these artificial hillocks. I have already noted the presence of faes beneath natural 'knolls' or 'knowes', so

23 Spence, L. *British Fairy Origins*. p182 & *Minor Traditions of British Mythology*. p144; Sikes, W. *British Goblins*. pp82 & 380.
24 *Old Statistical Account of Scotland*. Vol.7. (1789) p489.

it makes sense for them to take up residence in manmade features too. At Clunemore, near Blair Atoll in Scotland, there is a cairn marked with two upright stones which is known as the *Seltainna Cluana,* or the Fairy Hill of Clune. Another cairn, at Hetton in County Durham, is called the 'Fairy's Cradle.' Many such fairy inhabited ancient sites are recognised throughout Scotland – not just barrows but fortified dwellings such as brochs and dúns. These are often termed *sitheans* (places were the *sith* people live) but so close is the association between the *sith* and ancient monuments that a word such as 'broch' can often be understood to imply a faery hill, rather than just denoting a ruined prehistoric site. Another common term is *bruthan,* which Carmichael consistently rendered as 'bowers.' Examples of *sitheans* are found at Fowlis Wester, Perth (a barrow *and* stone circle), Carmylie, Forfar and at Kinross.[25]

On the Channel Islands of Guernsey and Jersey, the association of the fairies with the numerous megalithic monuments is especially strong. On Jersey many of the ancient sites are called *pouquelayes,* a term believed to incorporate the name 'puck'/*pouque.* It has been said that there were once around five hundred *pouquelayes* on this one, relatively small, island.[26] Many other sites have names linking them to the faes and the fairies are known to meet, dance and to play games at these *menhirs* and *cromlechs.* They may even have erected them, either as their houses or as simple monuments or markers. For example, a small

25 Evans Wentz. *Fairy Faith.* p172; Spence. *Fairy Tradition in Britain.* p319; Carmichael. *Carmina Gadelica.* Vol.2. p327; see too Spence. *British Fairy Origins.* p183 (Llanelli).
26 Poingdestre, Jean. *Caesarea,* 1889, 8.

fairy woman was seen carrying the huge stone that forms the *Palette es Faies* on Guernsey in her apron before she planted it in the ground. Interference with the ancient sites is obviously highly inadvisable. The attempt to build a church on the site of *La Roque des Faies* failed because the fairies removed the materials and tools every night. Eventually, the church was built elsewhere and the fairies were left to dance in peace at their chosen spot.[27]

Part and parcel of this group of ideas is an instinctive respect – even reverence – that many people have had for ancient sites in their vicinity. An Elgin man called Andro Man was accused in 1649 of setting up a standing stone and taking off his bonnet to it. He insisted to the kirk presbytery that it was merely a boundary marker, but they made him break up the monolith all the same. What's most impressive about this case is how very late an expression of respect for menhirs this was. Traces of older beliefs were still found amongst rural populations until comparatively recently, though. George Tyack, in his 1899 book on *The Lore and Legend of the English Church,* noted a belief on the Isle of Man that, if you pastured your sheep amidst a 'druidic' circle, the flock was bound to succumb to disease. In his *Second Manx Scrapbook,* Walter Gill mentioned standing stones at Germans and Michael that were called 'white ladies' and which were white washed to emphasise their ghostly significance. 'White ladies' are most commonly spirits associated with springs and streams, so this is a fascinating merger of ideas. On the Cotswolds in Worcestershire, there is a large flat stone

---

27 MacCulloch, E. *The Folklore of Guernsey.* (1903) Chapter III, especially pp125–8.

hidden in a small wood called the White Lady's Table. This mysterious lady dines with the faeries at the stone.[28]

The respect to the stones demonstrated by Andro Man is manifested more clearly in the many examples of offerings and sacrifices made to the faeries at ancient sites. On the Isle of Man in 1859, after archaeologists had excavated a barrow near Tynwald Hill, a local farmer sacrificed a heifer on the tumulus to appease the 'little people'. Earlier I mentioned too how milk is offered to *gruagachs,* brownies and other such spirits, either by pouring it out on top of burial mounds or on specially designated 'sacrificial altars,' not uncommonly marked by a hollow on the upper surface and known as the *clach an gruagaich,* the gruagach's stone. The libation would be accompanied by a propitiatory verse:

> "*Gruagach, gruagach,*
> Uphold my herds,
> Keep down the *guaigean,*
> Keep them from the *geige.*"[29]

The *guaigean* and *geige* are very obscure beings, but the names appear to be variants of the same term which denote a spirit that brings death during the winter. During winter celebrations in the Highlands a *Righ Geigean* (roughly meaning, King Death) was chosen by a community and children's rhymes refer to both the *guaigean* and *geige,* probably in the sense of a bogeyman to escape. In respect

---

28 Spence. *Minor Traditions of British Mythology.* p144; see also my *Manx Faeries* (2021).

29 *Manchester Times.* (April 2nd, 1881) p4; Spence. *Fairy Tradition in Britain.* pp57 & 319.

of cattle, perhaps the *gruagach* is being asked to protect the herds against illness and starvation in the lean months of the year. However, there could be other fae connections, as *geige* can mean a thin young female (very possibly a *bean sith,* for the 'slender faery woman' is a consistent feature of Gaelic tradition). Meanwhile, *guaigean* can mean either a short man or boy or a thick round cake. The former could be another *sith* being whereas the latter reminds us that oat bannocks were used in the Highlands to protect against malign faery influence.[30]

The reason for treating stones respectfully is simple: if you fail to do so, the fairies using or living at the sites will have their revenge. In *British Goblins,* Wirt Sikes tells the story of a Dark Age inscribed pillar standing on a tumulus at Banwan Bryddin, near Neath, which was removed by Lady Mackworth to adorn a grotto she was constructing in the grounds of her home. Her workmen were unhappy over this, because the mound was well known to be a faery site, but the rich and powerful Lady had her way. Soon after the grotto was completed, a terrible storm raged over the Neath Valley and a landslip completely buried her expensive new grotto. The *tylwyth teg* had spoken. This incident is just one example of a wider tendency for faeries to protect ancient sites from interference and vandalism with storms and other attacks. I mentioned earlier the spriggans of Trencrom Hill, in Penwith, who advanced upon a gold digger in a horde accompanied black clouds and lightning; at the cromlech of Mynydd y Cnwc, on Ynys Mon (Anglesey), there is reputedly a hoard of gold buried in an iron chest, but we may never know the truth of this

---

30 Carmichael. *Carmina Gadelica.* Vol.2. pp285 & 290; see too my *Darker Side of Faery* (2021).

rumour as the spot is guarded by the *tylwyth teg* who scare off anyone who tries to dig. A large block of granite, known as the Hoar Stone or Horston, at Humberstone in Leicestershire is said to be inhabited, or at least frequented by, faeries. A local farmer who broke off a part of it when ploughing was reduced to a poverty afterwards.[31]

Disgruntled faeries may exercise their malign powers, but they could also withhold their beneficial powers, which are often exercised at or through stones. For example, the ruined burial chamber called *Men an Tol* in Penwith in Cornwall has a 'guardian pixie' who can cure sickly children and, in particular, swap back stolen babies for changelings. In Scotland similar so-called 'shalgar stones', marked with a hole, were used in the same way. 'Shalgar' must be related to the Scots term 'shargie,' which means a changeling. At Fyvie in Aberdeenshire the shalgar stone was, in fact, two dolmen uprights placed with a very narrow space between them; babies were passed through the gap to help them grow and thrive. Similar such stones, at Hatton near Auchterless and at Noth, near Gartly, were removed by farmers, with unwanted results. The first pair were re-used as gate posts, but the man's plough horses refused to pass between them; the second menhir, the Drumal Stone, was used as a lintel in the byre, but the cattle continually got out. In both cases, the monuments were restored to their original sites to appease the *sith* folk.[32]

---

31 Sikes, Wirt. *British Goblins.* pp374–375 & 383; Hunt. *Popular Romances.* Vol.1. p48; Rhys. *Celtic Folklore.* Vol.2. p458; Spence. *Minor Traditions of British Mythology.* p143.
32 Evans Wentz. *Fairy Faith.* p179; Spence. *Minor Traditions of British Mythology.* p147.

Faery Fells

As I have already described, the faeries long ago took up residence in barrows and other ancient sites found in prominent and/or raised places – hillforts and other enclosures. This is because (it would seem) they were already familiar with living in distinctive or isolated hills. Take, for example, a conical hill with a flat top near Strachurin Argyll that's called *Sian Sluai,* the fairy hill of the host *(sluagh)*; the home of the fairy queen at *sith-chaillin* near Fortingal, Perth; the many *sioth-duns* (fairy hills) around Buchanan, Perth, or the conical knoll called Harry's Hill *(Tom Eanraic)* near Ardesier in Inverness, where the fairies meet at night and where changeling children would be left overnight, in the hope of retrieving the stolen human baby.

Across Britain, in fact, fairies have for centuries been seen either dancing on hill tops or disappearing into the hillsides. A Middle English text of the late thirteenth or early fourteenth century records this:

> "Þat Elvene beoth i-cleopede, and ofte he cometh to toune,
> And bi daye much in wodes heo beoth and bi niȝtes ope
> heiȝe dounes...
> They're called Elves and they often come into
> farmhouses,
> By day being in the woods and at night up on the
> hills."[33]

It is wholly unsurprising, therefore, to discover that many of the healers who were accused of witchcraft in Scotland

---

33 *South English Legendary.*

in the sixteenth and seventeenth centuries were alleged to have made their contact with the faes in hilly places.

Katharine Jonesdochter of Orkney in 1616 described how she had seen the trows "on the hill called Greinfall at monies in drie tymes." Thomas Leys of Aberdeen, and his lover Elspeth Reid, told their 1597 trial that they knew of a hill where they could raise a spirit in any likeness they chose. Katherine Ross said in 1590 that she "wald gang in Hillis to speik to the elf folk." A court heard in 1618 how John Stewart of Irvine regularly met with the fairies at Halloween on top of two hills near to the town. Isobel Haldane, from Perth, described to her accusers in 1623 how she was carried from her bed one night to "ane hill-syde: the hill oppynit and schoenterit in." In 1616, Katharine Caray was accused of having wandered amongst the hills of Caithness "at the doun going of the sun [and] ane great number of fairie men mett her."[34]

In time, in fact, it seems that the association between fairies and upland areas became so well-established that the mere suggestion that a person might have spent their time wandering around on hills might be a cause in itself for suspicion of their conduct and motives. In 1696, for example, Elizabeth Homer of Exeter was tried for sorcery. A key element of the evidence against her was that she had been seen for three nights in succession "on a large down in the same place..." Her presence there could only have been to converse with the fairies, it was implied.[35]

---

34 Goodacre, J. 'Boundaries of the Fairy Realm in Scotland,' in *Airy Nothings – Imagining the Other World of Faerie from the Middle Ages; The Trial, Confession & Execution of Isobell Inch, John Stewart, etc.* (1618); Dalyell. *Darker Superstitions.* p536.
35 L'Estrange Ewen, C. *Witchcraft & Demonianism.* (1933) p378.

From what we can tell, the faeries like particularly to live in prehistoric sites on the summits of prominent hills; I'll give a few examples from Wales. The Iron Age hillfort known as Bryn y Pibion is definitely a faery dwelling, as it features in a 'midwife' story; the headland of Dinllain, defended by ancient earthworks, was a place of fairy dancing, at the conclusion of which they would raise a sod of earth and descend underground; another midwife attended a fairy birth here too. Fairies gathered at the hillfort of Moeddin dressed in green to celebrate May Day and, lastly, the prominent rock known as Ynys Geinon was connected to Craig y Nos castle by an underground passage, which the fairies reached by descending a golden ladder.

A couple of other Welsh sightings further reinforce this association between the *tylwyth teg* and hill tops. The first sighting took place in July 1760, made by six people making hay in a field near Bedwellty. A very large number of sheep were seen to rise out of the ground and up into the air over the hill called Cefn Rhychdir and then to fly to another hill where they vanished. A little later, the faeries were seen to fly over the hill again, though some of the witness's saw them as greyhounds, others as swine and others as naked babies. A second case comes from mid-Wales in August 1862. Two carters, David Evans and Evan Lewis, were travelling from Brecon to New Quay in Ceredigion with wagon loads of timber. At Maestwynog, they saw some small people climbing to the top of a hill. These figures danced in a circle there for a while, but then began to spiral inwards, where they disappeared into the ground.[36]

---

36 Jones. *A Relation of Apparitions of Spirits.* (1780) pp11–12; Davies. *Folklore of West & Mid Wales.* (1911) p128.

To conclude, therefore, we seem to have a double conjunction of associations. The faeries were drawn to and lived beneath ancient stones and mounds. If those were also raised on summits – so much the better – as with the barrow called the Fairy Hillock at Carmylie in Forfar, which stands on the top of a hill.

Fairy Wells

Whether we're talking about humans or faes, water is needed for washing and cleanliness can, of course, be a major contributor to health. For fairies, though, water can have other healing properties.

In the fairy world, well water frequently has strong magical properties. In Aberdeenshire it was believed that drinking dew and bathing in well water on May 1st would protect a person against witches and fairies for the coming year. Hence the rhyme:

> "On May Day in a fairy ring,
> We've seen them round St. Anthon's spring,
> Frae grass the caller dew to wring,
> To wet their een;
> And water clear as crystal spring,
> To synd them clean."[37]

Faery wells frequently had health giving properties, and their waters could treat a variety of human ailments. Certain 'virtuous wells' were identified in the Wye Valley on the English-Welsh Border where fairies would dance

37 Fraser. 'Northern Folklore: Wells & Water,' *Celtic Magazine*. Vol.3. (1878) p7.

on Halloween, drinking the water out of harebells. These flower cups would be found the next day, withered and discarded, but if they were collected and dried, they could be used as a medicine. A local farmer tried to dig up a fairy ring near to one of these wells, in retribution for which the well dried up – but only when he wanted to draw water from it. The farmer then met a little old man at the well, who advised him to restore the sods – which he did, and regained his water supply.[38]

As well as curing many diseases, well water can help restore changeling children. The Well of the Spotted Rock near Inverness was one such. Weak or pining babies would be exposed here at night with an offering of milk, hoping that the baby would be returned by the morning. Similar such wells were known at Tomnahurich (on the 'Hill of Fairies') and on the Isle of Skye. In Northumberland, there is a fairy well at the foot of an ancient hillfort above the town of Wooler. It's also known as the 'Pin', 'Wishing' and 'Maiden' well and the practice used to be for young people to visit on holidays such as May Day when they would drop a crooked pin into the waters and make a wish. More importantly, weak children used to be dipped in the spring and a gift of bread and cheese would be left (for the fairies). We have here a fascinating conjunction of traditions, with the close association to the prehistoric site combined with the fairies' implicit influence over the future and over health.[39]

Given the health-giving qualities of well water, the offerings left at many wells across Britain were often seen

---

38 Eyre, M. 'Folklore of the Wye Valley,' *Folklore*. Vol.16. (1905) p177.
39 Fraser. 'Northern Folklore: Wells & Water,' *Celtic Magazine*. Vol.3. (1878) p17; *Denham Tracts*, Vol.2. pp151–153, also p143.

as being a 'payment' to the guardian fairy for the benefit received. For example, at the spring called Tobar Bhile-na-Beinne on the slopes of Ben Lara in Argyllshire, coins, pins, buttons and beads would be deposited in a hole in the side of an elm that grew by the well by those drinking the water. At Upton in West Yorkshire there was a renowned Fairy Well, the waters of which cured weak eyes. People came from as far as ten miles away to fill bottles, leaving in exchange pins or bundles of grass. On the Isle of Man, those drinking the waters of the well at Croggan would leave pins, buttons or silver for the fairies. At other springs, more elaborate rituals were involved, such as circling the well sun-wise before drinking and leaving a payment, even if it was only a pebble.[40]

The Isle of Man is a place much haunted by the little people, and there are, as a result, several 'fairy wells' known there. Typically, these are guarded by female spirits, such as the singing woman in yellow shining silk seen at Thalloo Holt. The well at Chibberna Gabbyl was the site of a fairy fair; at Chibber Vreeshey fairy music could be heard, and at Glen Cutchery, the well's water had magic properties that helped butter to churn.[41]

On the Shetland island of Yell, the trows would gather at a well at Arisay once a year for celebrations. They would turn the water to wine during the visit and the source was known for never freezing and for its clear, cold nature. Music was also heard at this 'fairy well' whenever local human women were in labour.[42]

---

40 Campbell, A. *Records of Argyll.* (1885) p123; *Leeds Mercury.* (May 5th 1882) p1 – 'Hazlethorpe Papers: Fairies'; Irwin. *Practical Guide to the Isle of Man.* p75; Gill. *Manx Scrapbook.* c.1; Spence. *British Fairy Origins.* p187.

41 Gill. *Manx Scrapbook.* c.1.

42 *www.tobarandualchais.co.uk* (December 18th 1972 & February 1960).

I have focussed on wells so far, but larger bodies of water can be held in equal respect. Thus, at Loch Shiant (the 'faery loch') on the Isle of Skye, coins and rags were offered to the spirits of the water. I mentioned earlier that annual offerings were made to the sea spirit Shoney by Scottish islanders, asking for plentiful supplies of fish and seaweed. A grislier story relates how, at Lochan nan Deean, near Tomintoul, a 'red-cap' living in the waters was once propitiated with human sacrifices. An attempt was later made by the local community to drain the lake so as to recover the remains of those lost to the faery, but he reacted violently, leaping from the lake, seizing some of the workers and throwing them into the depths, which then boiled like blood.[43]

Wells regarded as holy wells by humans might also have curative properties for fairies – perhaps indicating that they were originally magical wells before the church appropriated them. One such spot was the Well o' the Co, which stood beneath an ancient fort called the Dunnan on the coast at Portankill in Galloway. The well's waters attracted a lot of human visitors, which the farmer of the surrounding land, Sawney Adair, was unhappy about because the crowds trampled his pastures. One evening he was sitting on a little hill near the well when an old woman, dressed in green with a red hood, approached him holding a poorly looking child. She asked Sawney to fetch her the water in a stoop because "oor folk" could not go there – in other words, the holy water would do the child good but the fairy folk were unable to approach the well to collect it themselves. Sawney rudely refused to help her and threw the proffered stoup into the sea. She warned

---

43 Spence. *Fairy Tradition in Britain.* p323.

him that he'd rue the day and that he should never sit on her house ridge again; with which she disappeared into the little hill. Adair promptly regretted his manner, but it was too late of course and, sure enough, in due course everything went wrong on the farm – cows and horses died and the crops rotted in their stacks. Thinking back to the discussion in chapter two, we here see the fae control over fertility being wielded as a form of sanction against a human who has violated or disrespected a faery well, but this story also involves evidence of the faes living in small hillocks *and* in proximity to prehistoric sites.[44]

Given the glamour that lingers around wells, they are fairy places where care is still needed, whatever the curative properties of the waters. From lowland Scotland we have a story of a girl who sat spinning wool on a distaff by a well when she looked into the water and saw a pot of gold beneath the surface. She promptly marked the spot with her spindle and ran to tell her father. He suspected it was glamour intended to trap and drown her and, sure enough, when they returned to the place, the moor was covered in distaffs. Nonetheless, twelve men in green appeared and returned her original spindle with its wool all spun.[45]

The magical power of well water can be deployed against the fairies too. In the fairy-tale of the Green Lady, from Hertfordshire, a poor girl finds employment with a fairy woman as her servant. One of her chores is fetching water from a well and whilst she's doing this one day the fish in the well warn her not to eat the lady's food and not

44 Trotter. *Galloway Gossip.* (1843) p105; Maxwell Wood, J. *Witchcraft & Superstitious Record in the South Western District of Scotland.* p150.
45 Aitken. *A Forgotten Heritage.* p18.

to spy upon her. The girl ignores the second injunction and sees the woman dancing with a bogie. She's found out and blinded by her mistress, but the fairy well water restores her sight. In an East Yorkshire example, a troublesome bogle in Holderness was banished and confined beneath the waters of a well, since called Robin Round Cap Well.[46]

Fairy Rings

> "We'll trace the lower grounds
> When Fayries in their Ringlets there
> Doe daunce their nightly rounds."[47]

As I described in the previous chapter, fungi are closely associated with the fays – and, as is widely known, fairy rings have a poor or unlucky reputation. As one anonymous seventeenth century writer commented, rings are either the rendezvous of witches or, otherwise, are "the dancing places of those little Puppet spirits which they call eves or fairies."[48] This could readily be proved: set up a stick in a ring overnight and it would be found knocked down by the fays the next morning.[49]

Author Thomas Nashe, in his satirical pamphlet of 1596, *Have With You To Saffron-Walden, Or, Gabriell Harvey's Hunt is Up*, memorably mocks his victim by describing how:

---

46 Gomme. 'The Green Lady' Folklore. Vol.7 (1896) p411; Nicholson. *Folklore of East Yorkshire*. p79.
47 Drayton, Michael. *The Queste of Cynthia*.
48 R.B. *The Kingdom of Darkness, or the History of Daemons, Spectres etc.* (1669) p55.
49 Burne. *Shropshire Folklore*. Part III. p638.

"more channels and creases he hath in his face that there be fairy-circles on Salisbury Plain."

In a few words he highlights for us a fact that we simply don't appreciate today: that the former, unimproved landscape of agriculture looked completely different to what we see now. For Nashe and his contemporaries, evidence of fairies was everywhere. This confirmed the constant presence of the faeries for many; for others it provoked speculation about the processes of Nature that might generate such striking features.

Landscape Features

Faery rings used to be much more widespread than today, and they were also much more noticeable. Partly this was due to their distinctive appearance, but in addition they appeared in all kinds of fields except those sown with corn. Modern farming practices, with increased cultivation and use of fertilisers and pesticides, has drastically reduced the evidence, but we can still get an idea of what our predecessors would have seen in the countryside about them from the writings of naturalists such as Robert Plot. Discussing the English Midlands in the late seventeenth century, he described rings that were forty or fifty yards in diameter, often encircled by a rim between a foot and a yard wide. These rims might be bare, or might have a russet, singed colour. The grass within could also be brown but was more often dark green.[50] Plot sought to explain the rings scientifically, proposing that they were caused by deer grazing, by moles or by the concentrated dung of

---

50 Plot. *The Natural History of Staffordshire.* (1686) paras 17–27; *Leeds Mercury* (May 13th 1882) p1: 'Hazlethorpe Papers – Folklore.'

penned cattle boosting growth. Nevertheless, given their occasionally huge size and distinctness, and their tendency to appear overnight, it is unsurprising that others would readily suspect supernatural causation.

Welsh faery rings were described in 1831 by William Howells, confirming Plot's description. He observed within them several yards of bare ground with a patch of green grass about one foot wide in the centre – or else the grass inside was much greener than anything growing outside the ring. No beasts would ever graze within the perimeters, he commented.[51] Elsewhere in Wales, the rings were described as round or oval in shape and much greener than any of the greenery surrounding them. However, they were marked by areas that were red and bare, where the fairies' dancing had worn the turf away.[52] A ring seen at Fodderty in Ross and Cromarty in 1845 was described as a low mound of green sward surrounded by a well-defined circle forty feet in diameter. The grass of the circle was greener than in the middle.[53]

Lighting, Moles or Faeries?

The nature of fairy rings was comprehensively documented and their origins extensively debated throughout the eighteenth century. The *Gentleman's Magazine,* for a decade from the late 1780s, carried an exchange of correspondence in which readers described and theorised about these curious features in their landscape. Charles Broughton, writing in 1788, remarked upon the semi-circular marks that appeared consistently in his pasture

---

51 Howells, W. *Cambrian Superstitions.* (1831) p140.
52 Rhys. *Celtic Folklore.* pp176 & 245.
53 *New Statistical Account of Scotland.* Vol.14. (1845) p247.

land. They had a base of about four yards, he reported, and were half a yard thick (across their width). Another writer ('JM') in 1790 described the circles that appeared in the meadow-land near his home. They were six to eight inches broad with a diameter of six to twelve feet and were covered in champignon mushrooms. He noted that the land hadn't been ploughed for nineteen years and that the cattle were turned in annually to eat the aftermath (the stubble left after cutting the hay). Another letter from 1792 remarked upon the many large fairy rings to be seen in the meadows between Islington and Canonbury, north of London. The present-day inhabitant of the capital will smile wryly over this, as the area is now overlain by Georgian squares and terraces, built not too long after the letter was written.[54]

Both the writers just named ascribed the rings to mushrooms, but subsequent correspondents blamed the effect, variously, of horse dung, moles, lightning and, even, the Ancient Britons, who had dug defensive trenches on the sites. What we can tell, certainly, is that these very noticeable features in the landscape excited public interest and speculation because they were so common and so distinctive.

Most of the learned gentlemen musing on the formation of the rings dismissed the fairies as a cause, naturally. Robert Burton in *The Anatomy of Melancholy* (1621) recorded the different explanations, whilst seemingly hedging his bets:

"These [the fairies] are they that dance on heaths and greens as Lavater thinks with Tritemius, and as Olaus

---

54 See too *The Athenian Oracle*. Vol.1. (1728) p397.

Magnus adds, [and that] leave that green circle, which we commonly find in plain fields, which others hold to proceed from a meteor falling, or some accidental rankness of the ground, so nature sports herself; they [the dancing faes] are sometimes seen by old women and children."

Ludwig Lavater (1527–86), in chapter 19 of his book, *Of Ghosts and Spirits Walking* (translated by Robert Harrison in 1572), was sure the cause was dancing fairies, writing that:

"Olaus Magnus in his third booke and eleventh chapter *De Gentibus Septentrionalibus*, wryteth that even in these our dayes, in many places in the North partes, there are certaine monsters or spirites, whiche taking on them some shape or figure, use (chiefly in the night season) to daunce after the sounde of all manner of instrumentes of musicke: whome the inhabitants call companions, or daunces of Elves, or Fairies."

Evidence of Faeries

"… you demi-puppets that
By moonshine do the green sour ringlets make,
Whereof the ewe not bites; and you whose pastime
Is to make midnight mushrooms…"[55]

Whatever the scientists said, for generations of ordinary people, living amongst the rings, it had been well-known that the Good Folk were in fact the makers of the marks. In Devon it was said to be the hoof-marks of ponies that

---

55 Shakespeare, W. *The Tempest*. Act 5, scene 1.

137

the fairies rode round and round in circles at night that made the circles; generally, though, across Britain, it was the action of dancing feet that was blamed. For instance, Evans Wentz was told about a spot near St Just in the far west of Cornwall, called Sea-View Green, where the piskies could regularly be seen dancing on moonlit nights, looking like little children dressed in red cloaks. Another witness told Evans Wentz that the piskies preferred to 'play' in marshy locations and that these round places were locally called 'pisky beds'.[56]

In fact, a variety of fairy beliefs attached to the rings. It was widely believed that they should not be cultivated. Grazing them and, even more importantly, ploughing them, was strongly discouraged: a Scottish rhyme warned that –

"He wha tills the fairies' green
Nae luck shall hae;
And he wha spills the faries' ring
Betide him want and wae;
For weirdless days and weary nights
Are his til his deein' day!"[57]

Anyone foolish enough to ignore such advice would find their cattle struck down with murrain.[58] In any case, it was also widely believed that any attempt to eradicate the rings would prove futile. Ploughing could not remove them and they would return immediately, as was alleged to have happened with two rings in the churchyard at Pulverbatch

56 Evans Wentz. *Fairy Faith.* pp181 & 184.
57 Chambers, Robert. *Popular Rhymes of Scotland.* p324.
58 MacGregor. *Peat Fire Flame.* p2.

in Shropshire. It was said, too, to be impossible to cut grass from the rings, as scythes would go immediately blunt. In essence, they are ineradicable and uncontainable, as they keep spreading and getting larger and larger in circumference.[59] Hence, Restoration playwright Abraham Cowley described "A Dance like Fairies, a Fantastick round" the resulting rings being places "Where once such fairies dance, no grass doth ever grow."[60]

Just as those who interfere with rings will suffer, it was believed that those that cared for them would be rewarded: as the Scottish rhyme promised, "an easy death shall dee."[61] Equally, houses built upon rings were said to "wonderfully prosper" although one might have supposed that the trespass entailed in the construction would have evoked faery rage.[62]

An aura of magic and danger attaches itself to fairy rings, therefore. As a consequence, the tendency is to avoid them: in Shropshire people used to be reluctant to use those parts of a church graveyard marked with rings. To sleep in one is especially risky – you are at considerable risk of being 'taken' by the fairies.[63] For that matter, anyone who just stepped accidentally into a ring could be abducted by the fairies. Great fear about this danger was instilled by parents into children, who retained the dread into their own adult years.[64] The rings equally might be a

59 Addy. *Household Tales.* p134; Burne. *Shropshire Folklore.* Part III. p638; *Leeds Mercury.* (May 13th 1882) p1: 'Hazlethorpe Papers – Folklore'; Brockie, W. *Legends & Superstitions of the County of Durham.* (1886) p84.

60 Cowley, A. *The Complaint, or Ode to Dr Harvey* (1668).

61 McPherson. *Primitive Beliefs.* p97; Chambers. p324.

62 *Athenian Oracle.* Vol.1 (1728) p397.

63 Burne. *Shropshire Folklore.* Part I. p56; Richardson. *Table Book.* Vol.2. p134.

64 See, for example, Sikes, Wirt. *British Goblins.* p103 for just such a warning from an old Glamorganshire man and also Evans Wentz. *Fairy Faith.* p91.

place to which a person was 'pixy-led' and then trapped, as was recounted in the story of *Einion ac Olwen*.[65] The same story notes the distinctiveness of ring too: "a hollow place surrounded by rushes where he saw a number of round rings." If to simply step into a ring is unlucky, to pick a mushroom from one can prove fatal, according to the belief in Cornwall – and on the Isle of Man.[66]

There's possible piece of goods news though: May Day dew collected from a fairy ring is said to be excellent for preserving youthful skin. However, others warned that – as a rule – dew should *not* be gathered from rings (whatever the benefits for the complexion) and that the faes would counteract any magical quality it possessed anyway.[67]

Although far less visible than was once the case, faery rings are still a feature in the countryside. Fascinating and charming as they are, traditional experiences suggests that, even today, they should probably be approached warily.

65 Evans Wentz. *Fairy Faith.* p161.
66 *Northern Echo.* (July 12th 1894) 'Counter Spells'; Morrison, S. 'Manx Dialect Connected with Fairies' *Proceedings of the Isle of Man Natural History and Archaeological Society.* Vol.1, New series (1906).
67 Napier. *Folklore in the West of Scotland.* p157.

Conclusions

Despite the contemporary conviction that faeries are a kind of elemental being or nature spirit, the folklore evidence to substantiate this view is not strong.

There are undoubtedly close links with the land and natural resources, but a better conception of these might be to regard the faery population as being just like the human inhabitants of the same rural areas. They dwell there, they depend upon the land for their sustenance and, as a result, they are closely attuned to wildlife, to weather and to the seasons. This is a necessity to enable them to survive and thrive. However, no more that country-dwelling humans should we think of the faeries as part of the natural processes. They are deeply integrated with them, but they are still not part of the mechanisms of the natural world.

That said, it is undeniable that many aspects of faery life and behaviour are inextricably intertwined with their environment. Whether we consider their preferred dwellings, their leisure activities, their appearance, the creatures they associate with or the venues through which their magical powers are exercised or manifested, faery nature and power are embedded in the landscape and ecology of Britain. They may not be 'nature spirits' as such, but they are spirits whose being cannot be conceived apart from the natural world which they occupy.

One last word: given the present perilous crisis in both our climate and ecology, it probably should not matter whether we see faeries as part of the functioning of nature or just deeply attuned to it. Either way, if an awareness of their presence in the natural world supplies another reason to take urgent action to protect the planet, so much the better – for all of us.

Milton Keynes UK
Ingram Content Group UK Ltd.
UKHW020605240124
436603UK00010B/422